NIGHT OF THE LIVING DEAD

A new novelization by Sean Abley

Based on the film
"Night of the Living Dead" by George Romero
Screenplay by John A. Russo and George Romero

Night of the Living Dead

A Dark Blue Things book
Published by Dark Blue Things
5724 Hollywood Blvd.
Suite 109
Los Angeles CA, 90028
inquiries@darkbluethings.net

First edition October 2015

ISBN-13: 978-0692776032
ISBN-10: 0692776036

Cover design: Sean Abley

ACKNOWLEDGEMENTS

*Thanks to Hank Mishkoff and xBook
for getting me started.*

*And George Romero and John Russo
for the inspiration.*

TABLE OF CONTENTS

NIGHT OF THE LIVING DEAD

THE TRIP TO THE CEMETERY

The lonely country road stretched on for miles, twisting to and fro, the path dictated by the natural, undisturbed landscape of the remote farm community. Farmhouses were spaced far apart requiring a healthy walk just to visit a neighbor, and a vehicle for any errands, supplies, or — God forbid — emergencies. Small clusters of nearly leafless trees lined the poorly paved highway, rendering them equally as effective for shade or coverage as the infrequent electric and telephone poles. The early-evening sunlight's attempt to pierce the cloud cover was unsuccessful, relegating the otherwise featureless fields to a chilly gray color scheme. The air was still, devoid of movement or sound, but electric, as if something shocking had just happened, and now silence and stillness were required in the aftermath.

A lone car progressed down the highway, the dull brown exterior of the vehicle blending in with the rural surroundings. The metal behemoth moved a little too fast for its size relative to the width of the road, confidently straddling both lanes.

Breaking the speed limit and reckless driving were both ticketed offenses, but anyone who might care was miles away.

The vehicle slowed down, then pulled off the highway onto a seemingly random, unmarked turnoff. What was until now a too-fast drive on a desolate highway became a too-fast careen down an unpaved, single-lane road. The speed at which the car took the many turns, as well as its disregard for the vegetation on either side of the muddy thoroughfare, suggested the driver was more than familiar with the route.

Another turn and the car navigated through a cemetery, the driver no more careful now that gravestones lined the narrowing path. American flags, placed at veterans' headstones, flapped in the wind. The rippling movement caught in the corner of an eye might cause a visitor to think someone was staggering among the graves.

Finally the car came to a stop. Barbara, the young blonde in the passenger seat, looked out over the quiet field covered in headstones, flags, and plastic flower arrangements. Despite the long trip, she was still in a good mood. "They ought to make the day the time changes the first day of summer," she announced.

The young man driving the car was in less of a good mood. He stubbed out his cigarette in the car's ashtray. "What?"

"Well, it's eight o'clock and it's still light." Barbara pulled her compact out of her purse and began to check her makeup. Despite her surroundings — or perhaps because of them — she felt the need to look her best.

"A lot of good the extra daylight does us. Now we've still got a three-hour drive back. We're not going to be home until after midnight."

"Well, if it really bugged you, Johnny, you wouldn't do it." Barbara put the compact back into her purse to punctuate her comment. Her tone informed her brother she wasn't going to take the bait for the argument he wanted to have.

Johnny forged ahead, methodically removing his driving gloves as he fished for a confrontation. "You think I wanna blow Sunday on a scene like this? You know, I figure we're either gonna have to move mother out here or move the grave into Pittsburgh."

"She can't make a trip like this."

"I don't know that she can't," Johnny argued, searching for just the right tone to break Barbara's cheery demeanor, even though he knew his mother could never make the trip all the way out to the graveyard. Giving up for the moment, he asked, "Is there any of that candy left?"

Barbara opened the glove compartment and searched behind the maps and insurance card. "No."

Johnny reached into the back seat to retrieve the styrofoam cross they'd bought back in Pittsburgh. The cheap decoration, sparsely covered with flowers, inspired him to launch a second attempt at an argument. "You believe this thing? 'We still remember.' I don't. You know, I don't even remember what the man looks like."

"Johnny, it takes you five minutes."

Barbara's tone was stern. Had he found his way in? He kept at her. "Yeah, five minutes to put the wreath on the grave and six hours to drive back and forth. Mother wants to remember, so we trot two-hundred miles into the country and she stays at home." His delivery was heavy with the burden of the trip.

Barbara gathered up her purse and made a show of rolling up the window. "Well, we're here, John, all right?" Her pointedly casual tone was intended to put a button on the conversation. She opened the door and stepped out. The truth was, Johnny had won, her mood was spoiled. But she'd be damned if she was going to let him know.

Johnny took his victory in stride — there had been many before, and there would be many in the future. And honestly, it wasn't as much fun to keep digging once he'd hurt her. Much like eating when he was already full — it tasted good at the time, but the aftermath soured his stomach. He rolled up the window and started to get out of the car.

"Testing... We're back on? Oh..."

Johnny's attention was caught by an announcer's voice coming from the car radio, which he'd forgotten he'd left on after the broadcast abruptly went silent hours earlier. He called out the window after Barbara, "Hey…" then quickly realized the fact the radio had come back to life was probably low on her list of interests at the moment.

"Ah, ladies and gentlemen… We're coming back on the air after an interruption due to technical problems…"

Realizing the fact the radio had come back to life was also low on *his* list of interests at the moment, Johnny twisted the dial to the "off" position, and stepped out of the car.

Barbara was already fifty paces down the road. As Johnny made his way toward her, she turned up the collar of her coat against the chill, which was not just in the air but the circumstance as well. Cemeteries terrified her. They always had.

"There's nothing wrong with the radio. Must've been the station," Johnny chimed in as he approached her. He could see he'd been right: Barbara had no interest in the status of the radio, at least not now.

"Which row is it in?" She was well aware of the location of her father's grave, but idle conversation calmed her nerves. Without waiting for an answer, Barbara stepped off the path onto the lawn.

As her foot landed on the grass she felt… sacrilegious? Blasphemous? She wasn't sure, but knowing she was treading on the dead bodies that lay just below the surface made her feel as if she was breaking some kind of rule. Did they know she was stepping on their hallowed ground? This was a worry she always shook off as irrational — dead was dead, with no consciousness or perception — but still, she felt uncomfortable each time they visited her father's grave.

And, for some reason, this time felt worse than ever.

PAYING RESPECTS

Barbara led Johnny into the thicket of trees that populated the route to their father's grave. The branches, great in number and dense in arrangement, hung low, as if pulled toward the ground by a force greater than gravity. Their thatched pattern blocked the waning sunlight, and the brown leaves littering the ground would have been a warm harbinger of the impending holidays had they fallen on Barbara's yard back home. But here in the cemetery, in the darkened shelter created by the nearly naked trees, they just added to the thick, lifeless pall smothering the grounds. Even yesterday's light rain hadn't revived the dry debris. Instead the leaves were just thicker and more viscous, the ground softer.

Entering the silent, darkened natural shelter felt like walking into sleep. The long trip finally caught up to Barbara, and her internal clock shifted ahead several hours, all at once. Suddenly she was tired. For a moment she felt safe, protected by the foliage as if in a childhood fantasy. But in the next step, errant moist leaves shifted under her feet, causing her to slide slightly. Her momentary reverie pushed away, she was now fully awake and all too aware of Johnny's eyes staring at her back. *Don't slip or he'll say something.* As she ducked under the branches and made her way across the uneven ground, Barbara silently cursed her choice of footwear for the trip.

They emerged from the darkened thicket into an open section of the cemetery. The diminishing sunlight was brighter than under the trees, and it took a moment for their eyes to adjust. Now they were confronted with a maze of tombstones which had obviously been planned as a grid formation, but over the years had deteriorated into random plots dug wherever they could fit.

Johnny scanned the area. "There's no one around."

"Well, it's late. If you'd gotten up earlier..." Barbara said reflexively as she searched for her father's grave. As much as she resented Johnny's sport of needling her, Barbara rarely passed up an opportunity to chide him over even the slightest misstep.

"Aw, look, I already lost an hour's sleep in the time change."

"I think you complain just to hear yourself talk." The combative instinct was so ingrained, if you'd asked Barbara what she'd said to Johnny during this exchange, she'd have no recollection of her exact words. But unlike so many of their mini-arguments, this one was diffused by something of actual importance: her father's grave. "There it is."

Barbara took the lead again, guiding Johnny across the cemetery, this time to their father's headstone under an imposing oak tree. Years ago, in one of his crueler moments, Johnny suggested roots from the tree were probably slowly growing into their father's coffin. The resulting gruesome mental picture — tree roots piercing through the walls of the casket and into her father's face — was forever forcing its way into her mind. On cue, the macabre image popped up again as she approached the grave, but this time the roots burrowed even farther into her father's corpse, leaving him unrecognizable. Barbara's pace slowed at the thought, and she grabbed a low-hanging branch as Johnny marched past her, as if this friendly real-life contact might slow the imagined underground desecration for just a few moments.

Johnny, oblivious to the impact he'd had on his sister's memories of their father, jammed the metal spikes of the floral arrangement into the ground over the grave. "I wonder what happened to the one from last year?" he asked. "Each year we spend good money on these things. We come out here, and the one from last year is gone."

"Well, the flowers die, and the caretaker or somebody takes them away."

"Yeah, a little spit and polish, he can clean this up and sell it next year." This time Johnny wasn't trying to upset his sister; he truly thought he had stumbled across a moneymaking scheme. "Wonder how many times we bought the same one?" he joked.

Thunder rumbled in the distance. Johnny backed away from the grave as Barbara stepped in and knelt down. She placed her folded hands in her lap and stared at them rather than the modest headstone. Somehow looking directly at her father's name on the stone from this distance made her feel uncomfortable, as if she'd peeked through the open door of a room she was forbidden to enter. *Why does it feel so different today? I've been here dozens of times...*

"Hey, come on, Barb." Johnny was forever mystified by her reverence for this yearly obligation. "Church was this morning, huh?" Lightning and thunder punctuated Johnny's comment. No rain yet, but the sky could open up any minute, and he didn't want to get caught out in the open.

Another bolt of lightning and rolling thunder. Johnny dug his driving gloves out of his pockets and made a show of putting them on, hoping Barbara would take the hint and let them leave. The approaching storm was making him uneasy. Driving home in the rain was last on his list of preferred activities today.

A movement in the distance caught Johnny's eye. Down the path, in the opposite direction from which they'd approached the grave, someone moved slowly across the lawn. Johnny could make out a figure in a dark suit, but not much else. Something about the stranger didn't seem right; his gait seemed stunted, irregular. Suddenly, Johnny was keenly aware of being in a remote, virtually deserted cemetery. He looked around, half hoping to see someone else, even in the distance. But no luck. *Now I really want to get out of here.*

"Hey, I mean, praying's for church, huh?" he chided. "Come on."

"I haven't seen you in church lately."

Johnny chuckled at the thought. "Well, there's not much sense in my going to church." His impatience subsided as a cherished memory of cruelty popped up. He smiled. "Do you remember one time when we were small, we were out here? It was from right over there." Barbara knew the story he was about to tell and had no intention of listening to a repeat performance. She stood up, ready to leave, but now Johnny was keeping them from a quick exit.

"I jumped out at you from behind the tree and grandpa got all excited," he continued. "And he shook his fist at me, and he said, 'Boy, you'll be damned to hell!'" Johnny laughed. "Remember that? Right over there."

Barbara looked down angrily and walked purposefully past Johnny toward the car. Yes, she remembered. His cheery recollection of that day set her on edge. Something about his upbeat tone, mixed with her growing feeling of dread inside of her, made Barbara want to shove him. Instead, she just walked.

"Well, you used to really be scared here."

"Johnny..." Half fuming, half pleading, Barbara strode away.

The game was back on. All ominous thoughts of strangers in cemeteries were pushed aside in favor of Johnny tormenting his sister. "Hey, you're still afraid," he said with a gleeful lilt.

"Stop it now! I mean it!" Barbara picked up her pace, trotting away from Johnny toward the car. No more poker face. Yes, she was frightened. But more than that, she was angry with him for purposefully taunting her so cruelly. Johnny was momentarily stunned at her reaction. *Man, she really is scared...* Then a wicked smile crept across his face. *Just like the good old days.* And in a flash, the perfect parting comment popped into his mind. He laughed a little, impressed with himself. *What's more terrifying than the dead below your feet?* He put on his best late-night horror-host British accent and called after her.

"They're coming to get you, Barbara…"

THEY'RE COMING TO GET YOU...

"Stop it! You're ignorant!"

Barbara stormed away. As she stomped toward the car, Johnny gripped a large tombstone and dramatically leaned in for effect.

"They're coming for you, Barbara!" he called, practically throwing his words after her. He pushed off the tombstone and trotted after his prey.

She whirled around. "Stop it! You're acting like a child!" But Johnny kept advancing. Barbara turned on her heel and continued walking toward the car.

"They're coming for you!" Johnny called again. Then he remembered the stranger lurching in the distance. A quick scan revealed the man was actually moving toward them. They would have to pass right by him to get back to the car. *Perfect.* His initial fear of the stranger was replaced by glee at having another way to terrorize his sister. He pointed at his new friend frantically. "Look! There comes one of them now!"

Mortified Johnny would involve someone else so rudely in his ridiculous game, Barbara turned back to her brother. "He'll hear you!" she spat at him.

Johnny caught up to Barbara and grabbed her by the shoulders, holding his sister in the perfect B-movie-poster pose. The stranger staggered closer. "Here he comes! I'm getting out of here!" Johnny yelled, giving his best matinee performance. He made a show of fleeing toward the car, leaving a humiliated and furious Barbara behind. He stopped a hundred feet away to watch the inevitable collision between his sister and the freak stalking around the cemetery.

"Johnny!" she shouted at him as he ran away.

Not knowing what to do in this incredibly awkward situation, Barbara bowed her head and kept walking, hoping the limping man would let her pass without further embarrassment. After a few steps she realized their paths weren't just going to intersect, he was actually moving toward her. Was he angry? She was too self-conscious to look him directly in the eye. With her head still bowed, she half turned to him and gave him a nod, as if to say, "Hello" and "I apologize" at the same time.

And then the stranger's hands were wrapped around her throat and she was screaming for her life.

JOHNNY, HELP ME!

"Johnny! Johnny, help me!"

The man who earlier had been slowly shuffling across the graveyard now moved with startling speed and strength. One of the man's arms slid tightly over Barbara's shoulder in a terrible hug. His other fist clutched a handful of her jacket, trapping her against his body. What seemed so protective when she arrived at the cemetery would be her buttoned-and-belted undoing if she couldn't get away. Her attacker's face inches from her own, Barbara's vision was filled with his bloodless, gray skin, sunken eyes, colorless lips. His clothes were disheveled, torn. *He looks so...* As Barbara pushed against the diseased man he opened his mouth wide, releasing fetid breath that made her gag. He angled his teeth toward her neck, and she realized, *He's trying to bite me!*

Johnny rushed over and grabbed the back of the man's jacket. He yanked, trying to pull the assailant off his sister, but the man's grip was too tight. He yanked again and again, until Barbara finally slipped from the man's grasp. She half stumbled, half ran backwards to the protection of a large tombstone, ready to run away if she had to. Johnny would take care of this man. Then they'd go call the police.

As Johnny struggled to hold on, the stranger whipped around quickly, loosening Johnny's grip and bringing them face-to-face. Barbara watched in horror as the man tried to bite her brother, clawing at his face as Johnny desperately tried to hold him at bay. The maniac's energy never flagged. He was all clawing hands and gnashing teeth as he tried to gain purchase in the only exposed flesh on Johnny's body: his face and neck. Another swipe of the stranger's arm and Johnny's glasses flew off. Johnny concentrated all his energy on what he thought would be the last shove. The man fell to the ground, flat on his back.

Barbara felt relief for the briefest of moments before the man, as if spring-loaded, leapt up from the ground and once again launched himself at her brother. The men grappled in a bear hug, their strength matched in a draw until Johnny forced the relentless lunatic off balance. But the man managed to hold on to Johnny's jacket, and they both fell. There was a dull, flat *thud* as Johnny's temple slammed into the corner of a beveled stone grave marker. His body went limp.

Barbara's mouth dropped open in horror, but no sound came forth.

Oh…

For one brief moment, everything stopped. The world disappeared. She was alone with a murderous stranger and the lifeless body of her brother. Panicked thoughts flew through her mind in a split second.

But wait…
Is he dead?
Should I help him?
It's so cold…
If I stay he'll kill me…
What's wrong with him?
I can't leave Johnny…
I have to run!
Oh, mother will be devastated…

The madman crawled onto Johnny's still form. He roughly pushed Johnny's head to the side, baring the unconscious man's neck, and opened his mouth wide.

What is he doing to Johnny?

Before committing the unspeakable act, the man lifted his head and stared at Barbara with dead eyes.

Run!

Barbara backed away from the tombstone. Despite what every fiber of her being was telling her, she still hesitated to leave Johnny behind.

Go! Run! You can get help and come back for him!

The man stood up, his gaze never leaving Barbara. Lightning lit the sky. Thunder rolled across the horizon. Now that the man wasn't pressed up against her, the flash of light allowed Barbara to see his face clearly for the first time. His stare knocked the wind out of her like a punch to the gut. The eyes that bored holes into her were cold, dead… and hungry.

Run!

Barbara turned and raced toward the car. The maniac launched himself after her, staggering, moving carelessly but quickly.

She ran across the dead grass, then back through the thicket that was now an impediment rather than a shelter. She burst back into the open air and the fading early evening light. Now the car was in sight. *Thank God!*

Suddenly her foot slipped out from under her and she fell to the ground. She turned back to see her pursuer emerging from the thicket, swinging his arms at the branches like a wild animal but never averting his gaze from her. She tried to get up but she slipped again. *My shoes!* She kicked off her shoes, jumped up, and sprinted for the car.

Panic and momentum propelled her toward the automobile until she collided with the driver's side at full speed. She took a step back, yanked open the door, and jumped into the car. As she slammed the door behind her, Barbara's heart sank. She beat her hands on the steering wheel in frustration. *The keys! Johnny has the keys!*

She reached across the seat, pressed the lock on the passenger-side door, then locked her own just in time. Her attacker slammed his open hands on the window. Barbara screamed and instinctively blocked the glass with her forearms as protection in case the pane shattered. The man switched his focus and yanked on the door handle. Although the car was locked, Barbara grabbed the handle with one hand and held tight. The man alternated back and forth relentlessly, first pounding on the window, then pulling on the handle. He attacked the car with no regard for his own body. His hands and arms had become mere weapons, his own flesh and blood expendable in his pursuit of her. Barbara screamed at him, as if her high-pitched shriek was a physical force that could drive the monster away.

The man ran around to the passenger's side and continued his assault on the car. Before Barbara could slide over and brace herself against the window, he bent down and picked up a football-sized rock. *He'll smash the window!* Barbara pressed herself back against the driver's side door as the man slammed the stone into the pane once, twice, *crash!* Glass shards rained down on Barbara as she screamed in terror. The man dropped the rock inside the car as he tried to crawl through the window. Barbara recoiled as his hands clawed at the air, getting closer and closer to her face.

The brake! Barbara reached down and pulled on the brake lever. The car slowly began to roll forward down the path. Still avoiding the man's flailing hands, she gripped the steering wheel and guided the vehicle down the descending dirt road. *Come on, come on!* The car slowly picked up speed. The man jogged alongside to keep pace, clinging to the door via the empty window. *Let go! Dammit! Let go!* As the car rounded a wide corner, the increased speed and bumpy terrain were too much for the man, and his fingers finally released the window frame. He continued to awkwardly stumble and run toward her as the automobile rolled down the hill.

The car had outpaced the man by almost a hundred yards when Barbara looked back to make sure that he wasn't holding on to the rear bumper. As she did she accidentally turned the wheel ever so slightly. The vehicle veered off the path and slid up against a tree, stopping dead at the side of the road with a jerk. *No! No, no, no!* Barbara frantically tried to open the door, but the car was firmly wedged up against the thick tree, making the window unusable as an escape route. She looked back. The man was making quick progress toward her, aided by gravity and the downward slope of the terrain.

She slid across the seat and out the passenger door. The man was only a dozen yards away, practically tripping over his own feet in his eagerness to get to her. She ran down the road, ignoring the gravel digging into her stocking feet. *He can barely run. You can outrun him! Get off the path!* She dodged to the left, jumped over the brambles that edged the road, and darted into the woods surrounding the cemetery. The man followed her, severely hampered by the rougher terrain.

Barbara forced her way through the wooded area, branches snagging her clothes, her hair, her face. Tree roots and rocks threatened to trip her, but Barbara's terror gave her a strength reserved for those in extraordinary circumstances. Her breath and heartbeat filled her ears, but she could still hear (or she imagined she could) the man, that terrible man, chasing her through the trees.

She burst out of the woods onto the country road on which she and Johnny had driven less than an hour earlier. Without the uneven grass and brush hampering her, she was able to run at top speed down the paved, rural lane.

That man looks diseased...

...dead...

...killed Johnny...

No! Johnny's still alive...

...trying to bite me...

...biting Johnny...

She started to cry. Relief at her escape alternated with waves of guilt over leaving Johnny behind. *I'll get help and come back! I promise!* She gulped air between sobs, breaking into a rhythmic pace as she bolted down the otherwise quiet stretch of road. *Have to get help... Have to get help...*

Without breaking stride, she looked back, searching for the man behind her. He stumbled out of the wooded area. To her relief, he was more than two blocks away and advancing much more slowly on the flat road than down the hill in the cemetery. Even so, she knew she couldn't run forever. And what if there were others? What if he had accomplices? Was he an escaped prisoner?

The wooded area ended. Open fields on either side now buffeted her. *I have to get off this road. If he has friends and they have a car I'll have nowhere to hide...*

She darted to the side and ran into a field of tall grass and weeds. Her eyes scanned the area for something, anything that might help her.

Farmhouse!

At the far edge of the field stood a two-story farmhouse with a gas pump out front. She stopped running for just one moment. Should she? What if that was his home? There were no other houses for miles. Did he live there? She turned back and scanned the field for her pursuer. No sign. If he didn't see her hide there, maybe he'd think she was still running through the field. *They'll have a phone. No matter what, they'll have a phone...* She broke into a run once again.

Approaching the gas pump at the edge of the property, she stopped and surveyed the scene. The farmhouse, surrounded by large, leafy trees, was eerily quiet. Was anyone inside? Had they seen her running across the field? Deciding to try the door, she scurried from the gas pump to the front porch of the house. Grabbing the knob, she yanked once, twice. The door wouldn't budge. Not daring to yell for help for fear of giving away her location, she dashed off the porch to search for the back door. Her feet shot out from under her as she tried to take the corner too quickly. She tumbled to the ground, but a millisecond later she was back on her feet and running toward the rear of the property.

She stopped short just before rounding the back corner of the house. She still wasn't sure she wanted the occupants to know she was there. Cautiously, all too aware of how loud her breathing was –

Be quiet!

– she peeked around the edge of the structure.

He's here!

The man had circled around and was now approaching the back of the house, just a dozen yards away. *No!* She was now faced with the horrible choice: She could run away and hope he didn't catch her, or she could run toward the man, cut to the left, and pray the back door was unlocked. If the door were locked, he'd be on her in seconds.

Get inside! You have to get inside!

Barbara sprinted toward the door.

DEAD INSIDE

Barbara dashed into the darkened house, then immediately pivoted back around and locked the door. The man hadn't followed her, and she wasn't sure if he'd even seen her enter the property. But she kept quiet for a few more moments, straining to hear if he was getting closer. She leaned her forehead against the glass pane on the door and gathered her thoughts.

I'm in...

I'm safe...

... what if he gets in?

...and what if someone else is hiding in the house?

She turned from the door to discover she'd entered the kitchen. Typical farmhouse appliances and decor. Clean, tidy, everything in place — which meant no recent use. Exits on either side into different parts of the house, which was dark and completely silent, as if a thick woolen blanket had been draped over the roof. *If I turn on the lights he'll be able to see where I am...* Barbara tentatively stepped forward, unsure if she should venture farther into the darkness.

No one is here...

... unless they're hiding...

Steeling herself against... she wasn't sure what, Barbara stepped into the dining room. Again: deserted, silent, and absolutely spotless. This room was much larger, dominated by a table, with chairs and a couch around the perimeter, all perfectly in place. Whatever happened to the occupants, they hadn't left in the middle of a meal. On the other side of the table was the front door, useless to her now she was already inside. Despite the lack of an imminent threat, Barbara suddenly felt very exposed. The silence was unnerving.

She retreated back into the kitchen. As she stood in the middle of the room she realized the only thing protecting her from the maniac outside was a very thin door. *I need a weapon!* She opened drawers until she found the knives, then chose the biggest one. She clutched the weapon to her chest and backed up against the counter, eyes fixed on the doorway, convinced the man would burst in at any moment.

As seconds elongated to eternity, her thought process became more logical. What were her options if he did break in? She cautiously made her way toward the other kitchen exit.

She took a step, just a single step, into a sitting room. Nondescript furniture filled the room, as if this were where odds-and-ends came to die. She saw an entrance to what appeared to be a hallway with the lights on.

Even in the dim light she could tell some things were not quite right as she surveyed the room. A broken lamp on the floor. Magazines knocked off a side table. The out-of-place items implied... what? A struggle? A quick exit? The signs of life made the room feel less dead than the others, but no less dangerous.

As Barbara sidled further into the room, something fell against her leg. She jumped. A magazine had fallen off the side table as she brushed by. She released the air in her lungs, relieved. Slowly, methodically, she made her way toward the door on the opposite side. *A phone. They must have a phone...*

She moved out of the sitting room into the lighted main hallway. A staircase led up to the second floor. She could see into the dining room at the other end of the stairs. The doorway directly across from her led to another room, but the darkness on the other side of the portal prevented a clear view of the unexplored area. No signs of anything dangerous, other than the unrelenting silence.

Barbara walked straight across the hallway area and stepped into the dark room. As her eyes adjusted to the light, a tusked animal leapt out at her from the shadows.

No!

As she recoiled, more animals, wild animals with teeth bared and dead eyes, darted toward her out of the darkness. Frozen in place, unable to flee, her mind locked. All expression disappeared from her face as she tried to process this new, unfathomable situation.

I can't...

Oh...

The taxidermy animal heads hanging on the wall remained in place as she scanned the room, which appeared to be a den.

They're dead...

They're dead on the wall...

She was exhausted, not just from running, but from the nonstop sensory overload that began when the man first grabbed her. Like a prisoner being tortured, she was starting to shut down.

A noise brought Barbara back from her fog. *What was that? The man outside?* She darted over to the window, carefully pulled the curtain back part way, and peeked out.

The man was angrily flailing around in the yard, pure unfocused rage personified.

He's trying to get in!

As he neared the house, his arm caught on a clothesline, which seemed to make him even more furious. His uncontrolled thrashing yanked the rope from the side of the house and pulled the pole at the other end up from the ground. In his fury he hurled the implements aside as if they'd attacked him.

This scorched-earth reaction to what should have been a minor annoyance terrified Barbara. How would she fare if he caught her?

The man continued his path around the structure, apparently searching for an entrance. Barbara flung the curtain back in place and looked around the room. The man was actively trying to get in! She had to do something. If she could just find...

The phone!

She dropped the knife on the desk, snatched up the handset and dialed "0" on the rotary face. There was silence for a maddening second, then a strange tone emitted from the earpiece. Not the typical busy signal, or even a wrong-number alert. No, this was a pulsing tone, almost like a muffled siren or some sort of warning signal.

Dammit!

She rapidly pressed the hook a few times, then dialed again. Silence. Then the pulsing tone again.

No!

She squeezed the receiver in her hand, as if the plastic instrument was a living thing she could punish, then slammed the handset down onto the cradle. She ran from the room, more angry than scared. Then she remembered: She'd left the knife on the table.

Stupid!

She dashed back, grabbed the weapon, ran through the hallway, sitting room, and kitchen, and back into the dining room. She now knew that the layout of the house was like a life preserver: All of the rooms on the first floor surrounded the stairway to the second floor.

In the darkened room she once again searched for anything that might give her an advantage in this terrible situation. She moved over to the window and hid behind the curtain as she peered out. Was he still trying to get in? She gasped — the man was right outside the window! He was following her around the house!

As she tried to stay hidden, movement out toward the far edge of the yard caught Barbara's eye. She strained to see past the tree line, but the sun had almost set, making surveillance of the outer edges of the property difficult. But then, out of the darkness, just past the trees, two more strangers appeared. Barbara gripped the edges of the window table.

Oh, God...

They looked like average men, dressed in suit pants and jackets. But they, too, moved awkwardly, like the man from the cemetery. And they were headed straight for the house.

Do they live here?! Who are they?!

Barbara's pursuer turned to the two men. *Is he signaling to them?* He seemed to acknowledge them, but more as a stranger might acknowledge another stranger. One glance and he was back to menacing her through the window. The new men approached the house, as if they knew something (or someone) they needed was inside.

You can't go outside now...

There might be more...

You have to hide!

Panicked, Barbara leapt back from the window. She bumped into a chair at the dining table, almost dropping her knife as she righted herself. She rebounded and charged toward the main hallway.

She hesitated as she grabbed the banister leading up to the second floor. *Is it safe?*

Instinct kicked in, and she used the banister for leverage as she took the U-turn onto the stairs at full speed. But just a few steps in something told her not to rush, and she slowed her pace. As she carefully placed her feet on each subsequent step, she listened for signs of life. Nothing. The men outside made her want to move faster, but the unknown on the second floor kept her at a steady, cautious pace.

Another step. Another step. Barbara's eyes adjusted to the darkness just enough for her to see an indistinct lump on the landing. A pile of clothes? A bag? Slowly the mutilated body of a woman came into full view. She had fallen with her head at the top of the stairs, giving Barbara a direct view of what was left of her face. The flesh and underlying muscle had been torn off in chunks, leaving bones and raw meat visible. One eyeball was missing; the other stared, lidless, at Barbara. The lips and cheeks had been ripped away, leaving the teeth bared in a hideous grin. Blood, still wet, pooled around the stripped and broken skull.

Barbara screamed, the first sound she'd made since she entered the house. She wasn't thinking about being heard by the men outside. She wasn't thinking about being discovered by someone in the house. The guttural scream forced itself out against her will, as if she could scream away the mangled face at the top of the stairs. The grisly image was too much, too revolting, too out of context of anything she'd ever experienced. Her knees buckled. She staggered backwards, stumbling sideways onto the banister, which caught her midsection and saved her from falling back down the stairs. Her vision blurred, darkened. A black cloud crept in from all sides. She was going to pass out.

Johnny...

Her brother could save her. He was alive and just down the road and she needed to get back to him. She had to leave the house. She had to leave the house *now*.

Barbara willed herself back to life. She pushed off the banister and launched herself down the stairs. She raced through the hallway toward the dining room and the front door. The danger of the men outside was erased from her thoughts as she struggled with the unfamiliar deadbolt. She had to get out of the house and run back to Johnny. The lock resisted her first panicked attempts to turn the latch, but finally released when Barbara randomly exerted just the right amount of pressure and torque. She flung the door open and bolted out into the night.

Blinding light pierced her eyes. She stopped short on the porch and threw her hands up as a shield from the bright beams. A truck's engine shuddered to a stop, but the glare continued. She heard a heavy footstep on the porch. A figure moved in front of her, blocking the headlights. She blinked her eyes, trying to erase the light trails from her sight. As her vision cleared, the figure was revealed to be a large man holding a tire iron.

Oh...

BEN

Ben locked eyes with the woman on the porch. He knew he had only a few seconds to assess the situation before he had to make a choice. She seemed childlike, almost catatonic. She was holding a knife, but more as an afterthought than a weapon. *For now...*

She seemed more startled than relieved to see him, but she wasn't making any move to attack. *Is she one of those things?*

Her gaze moved from his face to the yard behind him. He turned to see one of the creatures approaching the porch. Two more were farther back in the darkness. *Just three. They don't look so bad. Not like the ones at the diner...*

A quick glance back at the woman told him she was as scared of those things as he was, which meant she wasn't a threat. *She's fine...*

He looked back at the nearest creature one last time, its arms outstretched, its mouth wide open. *Gotta get inside. Now!*

He stepped toward the door of the house, but the woman didn't move. He grabbed her by the upper arms harder than he needed to, but he didn't want to take the chance she might misunderstand his actions. And he needed to avoid that knife.

The woman resisted, but Ben's grip was strong. Before she could fight him off, he pushed her backwards and through the door.

Inside the house, Ben shoved the woman aside, then slammed and bolted the door. He pulled on the doorknob twice to test the strength of the apparatus. He let out a sigh. *Good... for now...*

"It's all right," he assured her. "Don't worry about him. I can handle him. Probably be a lot more of them as soon as they find out about us." Ben's tone wasn't so much comforting as perfunctory. He barely glanced at the woman he'd forced into the house. His eyes darted around the room as he took inventory. He quickly moved over to the dining room window, then looked into the kitchen. *We gotta board this place up...* The woman stayed rooted to her spot by the front door as Ben made his way back past her and into the den.

"Truck is outta gas," he said as he surveyed the room from the doorway. He turned back to the woman. "This pump out here is locked. Is there a key?"

Barbara offered him nothing but wide eyes and silence. *I don't know...* The assertiveness and strategic reasoning she'd used during her ordeal had drained out of her now that this man had forced himself into the house. Even her fight-or-flight instinct had evaporated.

Ben's tone became more pointed, louder. "We can try to get out if we can get some gas." Still no answer from the speechless woman. *Don't yell at her. She's in shock...*

He tried to control his anger. "Is there a key?" Rather than meet her helpless silence with a full-on shout, Ben gave up and stormed into the den to try the phone.

Barbara wanted to talk, but it was impossible for her to form the words she wanted to say.

Someone was murdered...

There's a corpse upstairs...

We were attacked...

She followed the man into the den. Maybe she could lead him to the dead body without having to speak the words.

Ben dropped down to the desk and grabbed the phone's handset. One "0" dial later and he was met with a strange, muffled emergency tone from the receiver. "I suppose you've tried this," he said over his shoulder. He listened for another ten seconds, hoping the sound would change, but no luck. As he hung up, he realized the woman had moved into the hallway. He stood up and followed her out of the room.

Barbara leaned against the wall. This was as far as she could go.

It's up there…

Oh, it's up there…

Ben followed her into the hallway. "Do you live here?" he asked brusquely. He was sympathetic to her shock — after all, he'd seen horrible things on his way to the farmhouse, and could only imagine what she'd been through — but enough was enough. The woman looked to the top of the stairs, then put her face into her hands and wept. Ben finally understood — she wanted him to go upstairs. *Well, at least she's communicating…*

He moved past her and cautiously climbed the stairs until he had a clear view of the butchered corpse. His stomach turned at the sight. "Jesus…" He stumbled back down, revolted by the bloody mess. He pressed his forehead against the wall and took several deep breaths. Before he found the farmhouse, he'd been caught in the middle of an attack on a diner by a group of men, women, even children, all of whom had appeared to be infected, injured, or just pale and bloodless. He'd seen a motorcyclist forced off the road. He'd seen a family dragged away from their car. And while he'd watched in horror and made assumptions about what happened to the victims based on what he could see from a distance, this was the first time he'd seen the unspeakable results up close. His stomach turned.

There was no safety here. They had to get out of the house.

Ben took another deep breath, then squared his shoulders and got back to business. He strode past the woman. "We've gotta get out of here. We have to get where there are some other people." He left the hallway and made his way to the kitchen.

"Maybe we better take some food," he called back. "I'll see if I can find some food."

Barbara remained in the hallway. Somehow the tight space comforted her. She couldn't go outside, she couldn't go upstairs, so she would stay right here. The man was so gruff, shouting at her, demanding answers to questions for which she had no responses. He knew what was happening and he wouldn't tell her. He just issued orders and stomped around the house. Well then he could stay out there and keep the men from coming in and she would stay right here. She would stay right here until someone came and got them. Or the police arrived. Or Johnny. *Oh, Johnny, come quick...*

She reached across the small space and touched the wall under the stairway. She ran her hands over the old paint, the molding on the stairs. The cool surface felt soothing against her palm and fingertips.

drip

Barbara's brow furrowed. What was that sound?

drip drip drip

She looked down. There was a dark, wet spot on the carpet next to her foot. Something was dripping onto the carpet. She looked up just as a deep red drop landed on her hand.

What?

She followed the path of the drop with her eyes up to the landing at the top of the stairs. Her eyes widened in horror as she realized blood from the corpse was now flowing past the banister and dripping onto the floor... and her.

Gagging, Barbara ran out of the hallway and into the dining room. She wiped the blood off one hand with the other, then rubbed her palm on her jacket. The feeling of sanctuary had been ruined.

It was time to figure out what was going on.

WHAT'S HAPPENING?

Ben searched through the cupboards for food that would keep for a few days, if necessary. If they somehow got trapped in the middle of nowhere, they'd need to eat. He dropped tin cans and boxes into a paper bag he'd found next to the refrigerator.

We'll find the key to that pump, fill up the truck, and drive over to Evans City. Take back roads. Avoid places where those things could gather… He considered leaving the woman behind. *She'll be no good in a fight. Slow me down. I'll send help back.* But he couldn't bring himself to abandon her.

Barbara stepped into the kitchen. She watched silently as the man gathered food. He'd left his tire iron on the shelf next to the cupboard, and the out-of-context object puzzled her for a moment. *Why is this here?* She gently picked up the bar and held it to her chest like a delicate toy, the weight of the metal innately comforting. The man continued bagging food, ignoring her. She waited patiently for him to explain what was going on, but finally she'd had enough.

"What's happening?" she asked.

Ben continued gathering food, carefully considering the pros and cons of each item in the cupboard. "I'll be just a second."

"What's happening?" she repeated firmly. Her resolve was returning, and she wasn't going to be ignored.

Ben stood up and set the bag of repurposed groceries on the shelf. He had to stop himself from shaking his head in disbelief. *Be kind... She must really be in shock...* He was about to ask her, "Do you really not know what's going on out there?" when the sound of metal being hit by a heavy object punctured the silence. They both turned and looked out the window.

Two men were attacking Ben's truck. One had thrown a rock, and now picked up a second stone and smashed one of the headlights, turning the truck into a cyclops.

Ben practically leapt over to the window in the dining room for a better view. He could see the creatures circling his truck. "Two of them..."

Barbara moved into the room behind him. Ben turned and grabbed her by the shoulders. "There are two of them out there. Have you seen any more around here?" He tried to coax the answer out of her with his tone, firm but kind. "I can take care of those two..."

"I don't know... I don't know..." Barbara could feel his grip tighten. *Get your hands off me...*

Ben was losing what little patience he had left. *Shake some sense into her...* "I know you're afraid, but we have to..."

"I don't know!" Barbara shrieked at him. She twisted back and forth in his grip angrily, hitting him with her fists. "I don't know!" she screamed again. *Don't you yell at me!*

Ben forced the woman backwards into a chair, then let her go. She began to cry. "What's happening?" she sobbed as he walked over to the front door. He didn't have time to be gentle with her any more. Let her have hysterical fits in the comfort of the kitchen. He had to get outside and deal with those... those things.

The two creatures moved on to the second headlight as Ben stepped out of the house. He watched as one man shielded his eyes from the beam while he clumsily heaved a rock at the truck. *They don't like bright lights!* The glass and the bulb smashed, and now Ben was outside, alone, in the dark.

The second man, who looked as if he were in his mid twenties with dead, sunken eyes and a ragged, bloodless gash across his cheek, staggered up to Ben, arms out, hands grasping as he neared his prey. Ben reared back with the tire iron and cracked the man across the face, hard. He felt the *thud* more than he heard it, the crunch of facial bones and flesh absorbing the blow simultaneously. Had Ben not seen what these creatures were capable of he might have felt sickened by inflicting this injury. But he had, and he didn't.

The young creature fell to the ground, and Ben immediately jumped on him, straddling his chest. He raised the tire iron over his head and brought the bar down on the creature's face, creating a bloodless divot from the forehead to the chin. The creature only grew more agitated, reaching up to claw at Ben. *That should have killed him…* Ben brought the iron bar down on the creature's forehead again. And again. And again. The creature finally grew still and his hands fell, lifeless, to the ground.

The other creature, with the same sunken eyes and several open wounds down one cheek, wrapped his hands around Ben's neck from behind. Ben turned at the waist and shoved the aggressor away, sending the thing sprawling to the ground. He immediately climbed from one creature to the other, pinning the still-moving attacker down and repeatedly smashing his head with the tire iron. The creature struggled, then lay still.

Ben wearily climbed off the stranger, finally convinced the man was dead. Exhaustion, caused by the fight and the events of the day, caught up to him in this calm moment as he pulled himself to a standing position. A quick scan of the yard failed to reveal any more intruders. He walked back to the house.

We should be okay now.

MORE

What's happening?

Barbara lay on the chair, crying. She hadn't seen what the man did outside, but the sounds, the sounds were terrible. She wouldn't let herself imagine what happened out there. She brought her hands to her face, as if her own touch would somehow protect her. But her tears continued to flow.

Her attention directed inward, she didn't notice the kitchen door open slowly. A man who looked like he'd been murdered, his throat slashed and a trail of dried blood leaking from the corner of his mouth, staggered into the house. Drawn toward Barbara, his unblinking gaze focused on her while one hand clawed at the air in anticipation of grabbing her flesh.

As Ben entered the front door, he saw the murdered man limp across the kitchen toward the oblivious woman in the dining room. Without saying a word he dashed forward and yanked her off the chair.

Barbara steeled herself against what she assumed was going to be another angry lecture. But then she saw the intruder over the man's shoulder. *His throat is cut...*

Ben spun the woman around and pushed her behind him. She cowered as he launched himself at the walking murder victim, bringing the tire iron down so hard on the man's shoulder he felt the collarbone crunch. The force of the blow knocked the weapon out of Ben's hand and onto to the floor.

Unfazed by the injury, the murdered man grabbed Ben with both hands. The two of them executed an awkward dance until Ben was finally able to force his assailant down onto his back.

Ben straddled the man, pinning him to the floor. The creature grabbed at Ben's face and gnashed his teeth, trying to take a bite out of his neck. Ben reached over to retrieve the tire iron, stretching his arm toward the weapon, closer... closer... *Got it!* He snatched up the metal bar, pointed the sharp end down, and slammed the edge straight into the murdered man's forehead. *Crunch.* Ben felt the vibration as the front of the man's skull gave way. The bar punched out the back of the man's head and embedded itself into the soft wood of the floor. The body went limp immediately.

Ben half stood as he yanked the tire iron out of the man's brain. The bloody head lifted up, then dropped back as the weapon disengaged with a wet *slurp,* hitting the floor with a dull *thud.* There was now a ragged hole in the forehead of the ghoul; a flap of skin and skull hung to the side like a dislodged plug.

Ben staggered backwards and leaned against the doorframe. *I've killed three men today...*

No, I've killed, but not men...

... those aren't men...

He regarded the tire iron, now covered in blood and brains, with disgust. But he sensed tossing the weapon away would be a mistake.

A sound from outside drew Ben's attention back to the kitchen. Another ghoul on the lawn, this one dressed in pajamas and a bathrobe, shuffled toward the door. The fact this one was dressed so differently from the others he'd seen gave Ben pause. *He looks harmless...* But Ben knew that wasn't the case. That thing wouldn't be here if he... if *it* were harmless.

Ben charged out to the back porch, tire iron held high. As soon as he was within striking distance, he stabbed the pajama-clad ghoul in the face, right below the eye. Once again the *crunch* of shattering bone reverberated up the metal bar as he made contact. Ben yanked the bar back, ready for another hit. He'd moved quickly, struck cleanly, avoided physical contact. He was in no frame of mind to analyze what he felt at that moment, but if he'd been asked to describe his feelings he might have said: "I'm getting good at this."

The pajama ghoul clutched his face and moaned, a low noise that sounded more angry than injured. He teetered backward, away from the porch and out of Ben's line of sight. Ben's heart sank as his newly unobstructed view of the backyard revealed four more ghouls. He bolted back into the house and locked the door.

Ben leaned back against the kitchen door. He hung his head in defeat.

"They know we're in here now."

DON'T LOOK AT IT

Barbara was rooted to her spot in the den, too terrified to move, too confused to make any sense of what she'd just witnessed. Who were these men coming to the house? Why did they want to kill her? *Did* they want to kill her? *Yes... the man in the cemetery wanted to kill me... These men want to kill me...*

She stared at the man on the floor, the man she'd just watched the other man kill. His throat had already been slashed by the time he walked into the house, yet she'd watched him walk, fight, claw at the other man's face. She'd watched the other man plunge the tire iron into his head and heard the sound, oh, that terrible sound, like a melon being punctured. And then the man died. Again. The other man ran away — *Don't leave!* And then she was alone with the dead man, mesmerized by the rupture in his forehead. There were sounds coming from the kitchen: a fight, a moan, the door slamming, the other man muttering something to himself. But the sight of the dead body on the floor drowned out anything she might have heard.

She took a tentative step toward the body, then stopped. *What if he isn't...* But the wound drew her gaze closer than her feet would allow. That small, deadly breach pulled her in, filled her view, until she was examining the hole so closely she might as well have been examining the man with a magnifying glass.

He murdered this man...

He saved me...

What's happening?

We have to get Johnny...

"Don't look at it!"

The dead man's head jerked away from her. She flinched, which broke her hypnotized stare. The other man grabbed the twice-murdered-man's feet and dragged him out of the dining room into the kitchen, handling the body as if it were an old rug to be discarded. Barbara grimaced at the lifelessness of the corpse. The only dead person she had ever seen was her father, and only after he'd been made over by the mortician and placed in his coffin. This body had... nothing. No life, no color. Once a man, now a piece of furniture to be dragged from the room. Barbara would have screamed at the sacrilege if a small piece of her didn't understand the murder had saved her life. *But is he really dead? What about his throat?*

Ben dragged the body through the kitchen. He dropped the man's feet and threw the back door open.

The sound of the door and the light streaming out of the kitchen caught the attention of the aimlessly wandering ghouls. Four of them were in the immediate area, but Ben didn't want to assume the visible threat was the only threat. He grabbed the feet of the dead man and dragged him outside. His intention was just to get rid of the corpse...

...it might get up again...

... but as he deposited the man at the edge of the porch he remembered something. Whatever these things were — men, ghouls, monsters — they didn't like bright light. Which meant they probably didn't like fire.

Ben retrieved a weathered book of matches from his pocket. *Thank God I didn't quit smoking...* His racing pulse and frantic mind (*Get in the house now!*) battled with his manual dexterity; lighting a match became a maddening task. The match finally ignited with a *hisssss* and he touched the flame to the dead man's shirt. The fabric caught fire surprisingly easily. Ben touched the match to the man's pants, which also burst into flame. Within seconds, the dead man was engulfed in fire. As he rolled the burning body off the porch onto the grass, Ben caught a nauseating, sweet, and smoky whiff of burning flesh. He didn't know what he expected charred human skin to smell like, but the smoke assaulting his nostrils was far more disgusting than anything he could have imagined.

The four interlopers in the yard shielded their eyes and backed away from the burning body. *Good to know...* Ben watched for a few more seconds to make sure the house wasn't going to catch fire, then hustled back inside.

Ben slammed the back door and threw the lock. He slid a small folding card table up against the door. Not that the weight of the table would keep the door closed if even one of those things pushed it from the outside, but he was operating on instinct. Anything that could impede the progress of the threat needed to be in play.

Barbara was in the kitchen. She'd watched the man light the body on fire, horrified. But now he was barricading the door, and something told her this man, despite his anger and aggressive demeanor, was on her side. He was doing what needed to be done.

Ben leaned forward, rested his hands on the table, and pressed his head against the door. He let out a heavy sigh. His gut was fighting with his intellect over the next move, and his intellect was winning. Unfortunately, this didn't make him happy. He used every strategy his gut presented as an argument against what his head was telling him to do, but he couldn't stave off the inevitable conclusion.

He turned around and sat on the table, his hands at his sides, his shoulders slumped. He looked at the floor, defeated. The lack of gas, the broken headlights. The strong men outside, the weak woman inside. The unknown threat beyond the houselights.

They had to stay in the house.

STAY INSIDE

Ben's eyes darted around the kitchen. *What next?* He spied a small toolbox on a side table and realized, *We have to fortify this place.* He opened the toolbox, but searching the contents in the dim room was difficult. He flipped on the overhead light and called out to the woman, "Get some more lights on in this house!" *Surely she can do that...*

Although she was still not used to having orders barked at her, something told Barbara she needed to do what this man told her to do if she was ever going to get out of this house and see Johnny again. She nodded silently and left the kitchen to turn on the lights in the den.

Ben pulled tools out of the box until he found a sturdy hammer, then looked around the cluttered kitchen for a likely storage place for nails. The hutch! He yanked open one of the drawers and dug through a lifetime's worth of debris until he found a plastic container filled with nails and screws of all sizes. He unceremoniously dumped the contents onto a shelf, then picked through the pile to find the largest of the lot.

Ben noticed the woman had returned to the kitchen, still in a daze. She stood in the doorway, leaning against the cupboard shelf, doing nothing except absently playing with the knife. The childlike blankness of her expression made him want to shake her. *Give her a job, something to do...*

"Why don't you see if you can find some wood, some boards, something there by the fireplace? Something we can use to nail this place up."

Wood? Where is there wood? Barbara was confused, but she wanted to do what the man told her to do. *Wood... Find some wood... Fireplace...* She stepped further into the kitchen, but her timidity caused the man to bark at her again.

"Well, goddammit..." Ben stopped himself. The hurt look on her face triggered his compassion. Yelling at her wouldn't help the situation. *Don't charge at her. Gently...* He understood. He truly did. Ben put his hands on her forearms and looked her directly in the eye. He spoke to her as if he were teaching a child.

"Look, I know you're afraid. I'm afraid, too," he said matter-of-factly. "But we have to try to board the house up together. Now, I'm going to board up the windows and the doors. Do you understand?" He waited a moment for that to sink in. "We'll be all right here," he continued. "We'll be all right till someone comes to rescue us. But we have to work together. You'll have to help me. Now I want you to go in and get some wood so I can board the place up. Do you understand? Okay?" The woman didn't respond, but he sensed he was getting through to her. "Okay?" he repeated. Her expression changed almost imperceptibly. He'd gotten through. She nodded silently. *Finally...* He gave her a slight push, propelling her back out into the dining room.

I have to keep it together. She's my responsibility now. I have to keep a cool head or we'll never get out of here alive...

THE ROAD TO HERE

Barbara passed through the dining room (*No fireplace... He said the fireplace...*) and into the den. The fireplace was next to the door, but her attention was drawn to a large, wooden buffet across the room. The ornate cabinet looked out of place under the head of the snarling animal mounted high on the wall above, but the bright lights in the room diminished the effect of the frozen, savage expression of the beast.

Barbara absentmindedly ran her fingers across the smooth wood, her task momentarily forgotten as she examined the piece of furniture more closely. The sole object on the flat surface was a small, hexagonal piece of art. Her touch triggered the box's internal mechanism, and suddenly the six sides of the gadget began to open and close in time to a delicate melody emanating from inside the device.

Oh! A music box...

The music was light and soothing, in contrast to the situation in which Barbara found herself. The tune sounded like a lullaby, but not one Barbara could remember having heard. The rhythmic motion of the small doors was hypnotic, and for the second time that day Barbara found her attention pulled toward something strange yet fascinating. She allowed herself to be lost for just. One. Moment.

Back in the kitchen, Ben gathered as many pieces of sturdy wood as he could find. He forced himself to think creatively, mentally patting himself on the back when he realized the heavy wooden pantry door, the type only found in older homes like this one, would make a perfect barricade. *I'll nail this across one of the more vulnerable entrances to the house...* As he pulled the door off the hinges, his eyes fell on an ironing board between the stove and the side table (*That works...*), and then on the floor-level bin someone had fashioned at the bottom shelf of the cupboard by nailing a piece of raw wood across the opening. He set the door down, then wrenched the board off the bin, revealing a cache of random pieces of wood, including some that looked as if they'd once been used as shelving. Perfect! He dragged the random scraps into a pile, carefully avoiding the occasional rusty nail.

Barbara's focus was pulled from the music box by the noise in the kitchen. She remembered the man had asked her to do something. *Find wood...* She looked around the den, not sure what kind of wood she was supposed to find. *Go to the fireplace and find wood...* She remembered now. Looking down, she found a small pile of kindling next to the fireplace. She scooped the wood into her arms.

When she returned to the kitchen, Barbara found the man balancing what looked like a heavy door sideways on the table he'd placed in front of the back door. The new barricade now covered both the middle of the kitchen exit and part of the small window next to the entryway. As the man leaned against the wooden slab, he fished several nails out of his pocket and put them into his mouth. Even though she wasn't exactly sure what he was doing, Barbara sensed he needed help. She set the wood she'd retrieved on the shelf by the cupboard, then moved over to help hold the door.

Without acknowledging her, the man took one of the nails out of his mouth and positioned the small spike at the corner of the pantry door. *Bam!* He slammed the hammer down and drove the nail into the thick wood. *Bam! Bam! Bam!* Barbara flinched at every impact, the volume of the act so jarring in this deathly quiet house.

She backed away as the man worked his way across the pantry door, attaching the barrier to the wall, blocking the window and sealing the exit shut. She was confused. Why was he nailing the door shut? *How will we get out?* This didn't make any sense to her, but she didn't want to make the man angry again, so she stepped back in to help. She tried to anticipate his movements, not wanting to bump into him as he moved back and forth to check his work, taking no notice of her efforts.

"They're not that strong," he said, she assumed for her benefit. He handed her a plastic container. "Here, I want you to pick out some nails. Pick out the biggest ones you can find," he said as he moved on to the second set of windows in the kitchen. She followed close behind him, dutifully picking out the largest nails and handing them to him as he secured more boards across the vulnerable spaces.

Ten minutes later the kitchen was completely boarded up. Ben tossed his hammer into the dining room, then reached in and flipped on the ceiling light, banishing every shadow. The woman stood in the doorway holding the container of nails as Ben grabbed a screwdriver from the toolbox and gathered up the few remaining pieces of wood in the kitchen. "There, this room looks pretty secure," he said, trying to convince himself as much as her. "If we have to, we can run in here and board up the doors. Won't be long before those things'll be back, pounding their way in here. They're afraid now."

The woman stood aside as Ben dragged the ironing board and wood into the dining room. Now that the light was on, he could fully take in what they had to work with, namely the ornate dining table dominating the center of the room. The table was almost certainly handmade, an antique, and Ben knew the piece was probably worth thousands of dollars. But he had plans for this heavy piece of oak.

He set the ironing board and planks against the wall. "They're afraid of fire. I found that out," he said as he rolled up his sleeves. Ben pulled each of the four chairs to the side, giving him easier access to the table. He gathered the empty place settings into the center of the lace tablecloth, wrapped the old fabric around the china, and deposited the bundle onto the floral-print chair next to the wall.

He shouldn't just throw those things down like that, Barbara thought. *It's not right. This isn't our house...* She unwrapped the tablecloth from around the place settings and carefully folded the antique material. The simple act soothed her.

Ben flipped the table on its side. "You know a place back down the road called Beekman's? Beekman's Diner?" he asked. The woman didn't respond, so he just plowed ahead. Truth be told, the silence of the place unnerved him. Filling the room with his voice, regardless of whether or not she responded or even understood, was preferable to the still, dead nothing. "Anyhow, that's where I found that truck I have out there. There's a radio in the truck. I had jumped in to listen to it when a big gasoline truck came screaming right across the road." He paused while he replayed the sight in his mind. "Well, there must have been ten, fifteen of those things chasing after it, grabbing and holding on."

He grabbed the hammer, but then thought better of bashing the legs off the table. *Too noisy.* He knelt down and searched for anything connecting the legs to the tabletop he might loosen manually. He found two large screws in each leg, so he took out the screwdriver and set to work.

"Now, I didn't see them at first. I could just see that the truck was moving in a funny way. And those things were catching up to it. Truck went right across the road. Slammed on my brakes to keep from hitting it myself. It went right through the guardrail. I guess..." Ben paused again, mentally tracking the driver's actions for the first time, grasping for an explanation. "I guess the driver must have cut off the road, into that gas station by Beekman's Diner. It went right through the billboard, ripped over a gas pump, and never stopped moving."

Ben was too impatient to extract each of the screws, so after loosening the first leg he flipped the table over completely. With a less-than-delicate touch he dismembered the heirloom, breaking the decorative lattice struts, and ripping off the legs.

Barbara couldn't watch the man callously destroy the table. *Why do we have to destroy these people's things? Why can't we just wait for help?* So she sat in a comfortable chair and stared down at the folded tablecloth in her hands. It was pretty, not like those men out there. Not like the burning body. Not like the table being torn apart in front of her. It was pretty and normal and quiet, and looking at the lace detail helped keep the ugliness of what happened on this terrible day out of her mind.

"By now it's like a moving bonfire," Ben continued, as he set aside the disembodied legs. "Didn't know if the truck was going to explode or what." Done with his first task, he sat and stared into space. Until that moment he hadn't spoken of the diner incident. As he finally verbalized the horror, images of the awful events filled his mind. The words flowed, unedited. He couldn't have stopped them if he tried. "I can still hear the man, screaming. This... thing is just backing away from it. I look back at the diner to see if there was anyone there who could help me. That's when I noticed that the entire place had been encircled. Wasn't a sign of life left, except..." As the mental snapshot of Beekman's Diner surrounded by a crowd of those monsters refused to fade, his voice trailed off.

And then he remembered when the screaming stopped.

"By now, there were no more screams. I realized that... I was alone with fifty or sixty of those things. Just standing there, staring at me. I started to drive. I... just plowed right through them." Ben didn't consider he might be scaring the already-traumatized woman with his story. The words needed to come out, and he let them.

"They didn't move. They didn't run, or... Just stood there. Staring at me." Ben's anger at the murderous crowd resurfaced. Their faces, their blank faces. How could they be so calm about what had just happened? About what they'd just done, for God's sake? Just standing there, as if daring him to do something.

"I just wanted to crush them." Ben remembered pressing down on the gas pedal, gripping the steering wheel so hard his nails dug into the leather covering. He remembered how, instead of running away, they leaned into the truck, arms outstretched, reaching for him despite the rolling death bearing down on them. And he remembered how the truck slammed into the monsters, and how he felt some of them grinding under the wheels as others bounced off the hood.

"They... scattered through the air, like bugs..."

WE HAVE TO GO GET JOHNNY

The man had talked and talked and talked, and then he had gone back to work gathering wood and tools and arranging the furniture. She hadn't really listened to what he was saying, but now that he was done Barbara wanted to tell him what had happened to her. Maybe if she told him, he would understand. Maybe they could unblock the door and run out and go find Johnny. He just needed to understand.

"We were riding in the cemetery. Johnny and me. Johnny…" Barbara thought about how Johnny looked after he fell. *No. You can't think about that. You have to start at the beginning. Make him understand…* She continued as if she were telling a sad bedtime story. "We… We came to put a wreath on my father's grave. Johnny and me… and he said, 'Can I have some candy, Barbara?' And we didn't have any. And…" Barbara was aware suddenly aware of the tightness of her coat and the warmth of the room and *oh, I'm suffocating in this coat…* "Oh, it's hot in here. Hot…"

Ben watched as the woman pulled at her coat's lapels and belt, struggling to open the garment while keeping the tablecloth on her lap. Her childish tone and behavior once again drew his ire. He wanted to be sympathetic, to give her the courtesy of listening to her story, but he just couldn't bring himself to do it. As much as he needed to share his experiences, what he truly needed was to get out of this house alive. And listening to her ramble on and on wasn't going to help him reach that goal.

Her coat loosened to an acceptable degree, Barbara continued her story in a singsong tone. "And he said, 'Oh, it's late. Why did we start so late?' And I said, 'Johnny, if you'd gotten up earlier, we wouldn't be late.'" The man didn't seem to be paying attention to her, which was rude. He needed to understand what happened to her and Johnny. She leaned forward and spoke directly to him.

"Johnny asked me if I were afraid. And I said, 'I'm not afraid, Johnny.'" Barbara was getting to the important part, but the man kept moving around the room, ignoring her as he worked. She spoke more forcefully. "And then this man started walking up the road. He came slowly, and Johnny kept teasing me and saying, 'He's coming to get you, Barbara.' And I laughed at him, and said, 'Johnny, stop it.'" Barbara's voice was anything but jovial now. Her rueful tone reflected her anger at Johnny's teasing. As she remembered the horrific afternoon encounter in more and more detail, she became both more agitated and more didactic at the same time. "And then Johnny ran away. And I went up to this man, and I was going to apologize..."

Why can't she just shut up? "Why don't you just keep calm?" Ben asked as he hefted the heavy table top to a leaning position against the wall.

She ignored him. "And I looked up, and I said, 'Good evening,' and he grabbed me!" Barbara started to shout. "He grabbed me! And he ripped at me!" The memory, still raw, took over. She was no longer telling a story but reliving the assault from her chair, angrily pulling at her clothes, as if she were both attacker and victim. "He held me and he ripped at my clothes!"

"I think you should just calm down," Ben said firmly. Her hysteria was going to draw those things to the house...

"Oh, I screamed, 'Johnny! Johnny, help me! Oh, help me!' And he wouldn't let me go! He ripped... And then Johnny came..." She stopped fighting herself as she remembered how Johnny had raced to her aid. Her voice was filled with admiration for her brave brother. "And he ran and he... he fought this man. And I got so afraid I ran." She began to cry. "I ran... I ran... And Johnny didn't come."

Ben completely tuned the woman out. She was of no use to him in her hysterical state, and listening to her story wasn't going to help him get the house boarded up. He ignored her and continued organizing their supplies.

Barbara's memories finally carried her from the cemetery to the farmhouse, and she realized where she was. The man was boarding up the house, but if he did that Johnny wouldn't be able to get in. "We've got... We have to wait for Johnny." He needed to wait, but the man wouldn't stop moving the wood planks around the house. She tried again. "Maybe... we'd better go out and get him," she asserted. "We have to go out and get Johnny. He's out there!" she begged. The man ignored her. What did she have to do to make him understand? Her anger rose. "Please, don't you hear me? We've got to go out and get him! Please!" Barbara was yelling now, frantic. She leapt out of the chair and inserted herself between the man and his precious pile of boards. "We have got to go get Johnny! Please help me!" She grabbed him by the arm and yanked him away from the door. "Please!" she shrieked at him.

Ben was forced to deal with the crazed woman, but he was done being nice. "Look, don't you know what's going on out there?" he asked. "This is no Sunday-school picnic!"

Barbara grabbed the man by the shoulders and shook him. "Don't you understand?" she screamed. "My brother is alone!"

Ben grabbed the woman by the wrists and held her at bay. *Calm but firm. She has to understand.* "Your brother is dead," he said evenly.

Barbara yanked her hands out of the man's grip, furious. "No! My brother is not dead!" She dove for the front door and pulled on the handle. She was not going to let him keep her from Johnny.

Ben grabbed the woman and yanked her away from the door. He wasn't going to let her get them both killed. If he had to stop her physically, so be it. He shoved her backwards and maneuvered himself so he stood between her and the doorway. She bared her teeth at him in anger, her expression feral, seething. Before he could stop her, she slapped him, hard. Without a second's hesitation, Ben balled his hand into a fist and punched her in the face. She recoiled to the side, bent over at the waist.

He hit me...

Barbara turned to look at the man, stunned. She saw a shocked look on his face, then dark curtains closed over her eyes and she lost consciousness.

Ben reached out and caught the woman as she collapsed. *I had to do it. She was going to get us killed.* He hadn't enjoyed hitting her, but he was willing to do whatever was necessary to keep them safe. Maybe she would understand when she woke up.

Ben swept his arm under the unconscious woman's knees and picked her up. She was light, delicate. For a moment he regretted taking his aggression out on this frail woman. He placed her on the couch, then unbelted and unbuttoned her coat to make her more comfortable.

Finally, he could work in peace.

THE RADIO

Fifteen minutes later, Ben had nearly finished boarding up the dining room, which included using the heavy table top to block the largest window facing the front yard. With the house now silent, he realized what he'd been missing since leaving the truck and entering the house: a news broadcast. He'd listened to the local news while driving to the farm house, but the reporters didn't seem to know much more about what was going on than he did. But now hours had passed, and surely there would be something about the attack on the diner, at the very least.

Ben hadn't seen a television in the house, but there was a freestanding, antique radio in the den. He knelt in front of the console and turned the power knob to "On." Waiting for the old tubes to warm up forced Ben to take a moment and do nothing, a luxury he didn't feel he could afford. When a high-pitched theremin-like sound squealed from the speakers, he immediately twisted the knob back and forth, searching for a station. The dial brushed past a millisecond-long blip of a live voice, so he inched the knob backwards, finally lining up the needle with the sweet spot of a news broadcast.

"Because of the obvious threat to untold numbers of citizens, and because of the crisis which is even now developing, this radio station will remain on the air, day and night. This station and hundreds of other radio and TV stations throughout this part of the country are pooling their resources through an emergency network hookup to keep you informed of all developments."

Ben returned to the dining room. He needed to put the last few nails into the tabletop blocking the window, but he kept one ear on the news.

"At this hour, we repeat, these are the facts as we know them. There is an epidemic of mass murder being committed by a virtual army of unidentified assassins. The murders are taking place in villages, cities, rural homes, and suburbs with no apparent pattern or reason for the slayings. It seems to be a sudden, general explosion of mass homicide. We have some descriptions of the assassins. Eyewitnesses say they are ordinary looking people. Some say they appear to be in a kind of trance. Others describe them as being..."

Ben's focus on the radio was shattered when he peeked outside. The men, creatures, "unidentified assassins" as per the newscaster, were regrouping outside by the truck. *If enough of them show up, they could roll that truck. Time for more fire...*

"So, at this point there is no really authentic way for us to say who or what to look for, and guard yourself against misshapen monsters."

Ben moved quickly back into the den. He grabbed a box of wooden matches from the hearth above the fireplace. He was about to strike a match when he realized there was no wood in sight. *Dammit!* He yanked open the closet door beside the fireplace and found not only a box of firewood, but a can of lighter fluid as well. He pulled the box out and knelt on the stone apron surrounding the grate.

"Reaction of law-enforcement officials is one of complete bewilderment at this hour. Police, sheriffs' deputies, and emergency ambulances are literally deluged with calls for help. The scene can best be described as mayhem."

Ben tossed several pieces of wood into the fireplace. He didn't have time to light the fire properly with kindling, so he doused the pile with lighter fluid. Striking a match, he touched the business end to the combustible liquid. The wood instantly burst into flames. *You never know... They might try to climb down the chimney...* Ben snatched up the matches and the lighter fluid and hustled back into dining room.

"Mayors of Pittsburgh, Philadelphia, and Miami, along with the governors of several eastern and Midwestern states, have indicated the National Guard may be mobilized at any moment, but that has not happened as yet."

After taking stock of his options in the dining room, he decided on the chair in the corner by the window, the same chair in which the woman sat as she tried to tell him the story about her late brother. He pulled the heavy, overstuffed seat away from the wall to a position directly in front of the porch door. He opened the lighter fluid and shook the can over the chair. The liquid came out frustratingly slow, so he squeezed the container. The fluid shot out in a stream, soaked the thick fabric, and filled the air with the sharp, acrid smell of gasoline.

"The only advice our reporters have been able to get from official sources is for private citizens to stay in their homes behind locked doors. Do not venture outside, for any reason, until the nature of this crisis has been determined and until we can advise what course of action to take."

Sorry, buddy, if I don't venture outside and take care of business, those things are gonna venture right in after us. Ben was ready to put his plan into action, but he still needed a more reliable source of flame than his book of matches. Inspired by the old, cotton draperies hanging over the window by the door, he grabbed one and tugged. The cheap fabric gave way easily, barely rattling the rod. Ben tore the curtain in two, creating six-inch-wide strips as he pulled the pieces apart. Picking up one of the heavy table legs he'd tossed aside, he wrapped a strip around the thick end.

"Keep listening to radio and TV for any special instructions as this crisis develops further. Thousands of office and factory workers are being urged to stay at their places of employment, not to make any attempt to get to their homes. However, in spite of this urging and warning, streets and highways are packed with frantic people trying to reach their families, or apparently to flee just anywhere."

Ben dashed back into the den and jammed the dry table leg into the fireplace. The curtain fabric lit instantly, surprising Ben with the size of the flames. He suddenly realized how dangerous this maneuver was. If he was careless and accidentally let the flames reach the walls, ceiling, or any of the furniture, the old house would go up in a heartbeat, forcing them out into the arms of the things in the darkness. Fighting his urge to work faster, he cautiously walked the torch back into the dining room.

"Repeat: The safest course of action at this time is simply to stay where you are…"

Ben cursed himself when he realized that he'd left a pile of planks and the ironing board leaning up against the door, all dry as a bone and ready to go up in flames. *Dammit!* Holding the torch to the side with one hand, he unceremoniously swept the boards to the floor with the other. He took a moment to position

himself between the chair and the door. *On the count of three...
One, two...*

Yanking the door open with his free hand, he reached over
and grabbed the starter-fluid-soaked chair, making sure he
didn't prematurely torch the flammable material before he got
outside.

He charged out of the house, torch held high, chair in front
of him like a shield. The ghouls by the truck turned toward him,
their attention momentarily drawn away from destroying the
vehicle. The number of monsters had risen, with four clearly
visible by the truck, and more, perhaps five, six, lurking in the
shadows beyond the trees. Ben thought he glimpsed a naked
woman staggering among the men, the first female ghoul he'd
seen since the attack at the diner.

He shoved the chair as far out as he dared, then he touched
the flaming table leg to the surface. With a *whomp* Ben felt
more than heard, the fabric was instantly engulfed in flames.
Damn! Ben was suddenly keenly aware a torch and chair were
burning faster than he'd anticipated on the porch of an old,
wooden farmhouse. Using his foot, Ben pushed the burning
chair toward the ghouls. *Take that, you sons of bitches...*

As the blazing barricade tumbled down the stairs, the closest
killers threw up their arms, shielding their faces from the
flames. To Ben's dismay, the chair's trajectory ended mere feet
from the porch, with the flames lapping dangerously close to the
old wood. *Goddammit!* There was nothing he could do now, so
he threw the torch out onto the yard and watched the ghouls as
they staggered back to avoid the fire.

*That should keep them away for a while. But how long will
it be until there are too many of them to shoo away with a
burning chair?*

BOARDED UP

Ben slammed the door behind him, picked up his hammer, and grabbed a board. He wanted to take advantage of the fact the ghouls were so preoccupied with the fire the noisy work of barricading the windows wouldn't attract their attention. He'd been nailing boards to the walls regardless, but he appreciated the added security of this moment.

Now that he was back in the house, he could once again hear the radio.

"Ladies and gentlemen, we've just received word that the President has called a meeting of his Cabinet to deal with the sudden epidemic of murder which has seized the eastern third of this nation. The meeting is scheduled to convene within the hour. Members of the Presidential Cabinet will be joined by officials of the FBI and the Joint Chiefs behind closed doors. A White House spokesman, in announcing this conference, says there will be an official announcement as soon as possible following that meeting. This is the latest dispatch just received in our newsroom."

The radio announcer droned on and on, filling airtime by repeating the same information over and over again with minor embellishments here and there in an attempt to vary his cadence. Now that he better grasped the situation playing out across the country, the newscaster was able to squelch the horror from his voice. His professionalism kicked in, and he instinctively added a slight thrill to his tone, a trick broadcasters employed to keep audiences tuned in with the promise of, "This can only get more exciting!"

But none of that worked on Ben. Soon the program became mere background noise as he continued his task of transforming the house into a fortress.

"Latest word also from national press services in Washington, D.C. now tells us that the emergency Presidential conference which we've just mentioned will include high-ranking scientists from National Aeronautics and Space Administration."

Soon Ben had secured the dining room with boards covering every possible entryway. As he surveyed his work, he realized the woman was still motionless on the dining room sofa. She'd slept through everything; his punch might have knocked her out, but her body subsequently shut down in its own defense. No one could have slept through the racket he'd made unless they desperately needed to.

Sitting room next... He picked up a door he'd pulled from another closet and headed toward the center hallway connecting the dining room, den, stairway, and sitting room. As he hefted the large slab of wood, he realized there was another door he'd forgotten: the door to the center hallway. *Great. That's one more, plus the closet in the sitting room, doors in the hallway, plus whatever we find upstairs. I just hope we don't run out of nails...*

"Radio and TV stations across the eastern part of the country, including the one to which you are listening, have

joined their facilities in an emergency network to bring you this news as it develops."

On his way out of the dining room, Ben brushed by the center hallway door. If he'd taken the time to investigate, he would have discovered what appeared to be the outline of a passageway cut into the wall behind that door. A small sliding bolt had been added to lock the rudimentary entryway from the dining-room side, but at the moment that bolt was in the unlocked position. Considering its placement, one might assume this portal led to a basement.

In the center hallway, Ben jammed a screwdriver into the top hinge of the den's doorway. He pounded at the handle with his hammer until the hardware started to give way.

The noise finally penetrated the fog surrounding Barbara. The sound of a hammer approached her from a distance, growing closer and closer, filling her brain, lifting her from slumber into consciousness. *What?* Between the blows of the hammer, a voice, a man's voice, clipped, staccato, worked its way into her ears.

"We urge you to stay tuned to radio and TV and to stay indoors at all costs..."

But Johnny said the radio was broken...

Pain in her jaw joined the hammering and the voice to drag her from sleep. *Ow...*

She opened her eyes. Her vision was filled with a yellowed ceiling, cracking from age and covered in cobwebs. She brought her hand up to her face, as if the touch could ease the pain.

"Late reports reaching this newsroom tell of frightened people seeking refuge in churches, schools, and government buildings, demanding shelter and protection from the wholesale murder which apparently is engulfing much of the nation."

Murder? Barbara pulled herself up. She'd been asleep, but didn't feel rested. The world was still fuzzy, muted, despite the voice and the hammer. *Where is that voice coming from?*

"Law-enforcement officials are at a loss to explain or, even at this hour, even to theorize about the reasons for this wave of murder..."

The hammering stopped, but the voice continued. She allowed herself the gift of not caring while she searched her memory for what happened before she'd fallen asleep.

Ben stepped down from the couch on which he'd been standing while he boarded up the last window in the sitting room. He needed to take a break, smoke a cigarette. As he dropped down to sit on the sofa, the window shade he'd propped against the wall fell behind him. Ben angrily yanked the crumpled blind from the couch and tossed the contraption onto the floor. He really needed that smoke.

The radio broadcast floated into the room as Ben pulled out a pack of cigarettes.

"Chief T.K. Dunmore of Camden, North Carolina, is quoted as saying, quote, 'Tell the people, for God's sake, to get off the streets. Tell 'em to go home and lock their doors and windows up tight. We don't know what kind of murder-happy characters we have here.' End quote. That's Chief Dunmore of Camden, North Carolina."

The first drag on the cigarette sent soothing nicotine into Ben's lungs. *I'll give it up if we get out of here alive. Swear to God...* He took a few more puffs while he surveyed the room. He hadn't spent much time there yet, and the contents were still new to him. *That closet...*

"So far the only descriptions, the only clues anyone has of the killers, come from frightened witnesses. These eyewitness

accounts variously describe the murderers as 'ordinary looking people,' 'misshapen monsters,' 'people who look like they're in a trance,' and 'things that look like people but act like animals.'"

Ben rose from the couch and moved over to the closet. He stuck the cigarette in his lips and pulled open the door. The contents were a jumble of worn-out clothes, unmarked boxes, household items that looked like they had nowhere else to go. He mentally cataloged what he could, but stopped when his gaze fell on a pile of women's shoes. Two pairs of high heels and a dirty pair of flats that looked as if they'd been worn while gardening were nestled in among some old blankets on the floor. The sight sparked a memory. *She needs shoes. She'll need shoes if we have to run for it...* Ben chose the flats, which seemed to be the most practical items in the closet...

And then he saw the gun.

"Some eyewitnesses tell of seeing victims who look as though they had been torn apart. This whole ghastly story began developing two days ago with the report of the slaying of a family of seven. Since then, reports of some senseless killings began snowballing in a reign of terror which has hopscotched..."

Ben tossed the shoes aside and snatched up the weapon. *Of course they have a shotgun! Probably more than one around here somewhere...* He'd held a gun before. He'd even *shot* a gun before. But this was the first time he'd actually been relieved to have a gun in his hands. For the first time in this whole ordeal Ben felt he was in control, as if by holding the gun he was claiming the house as his own.

Bullets... After he carefully stubbed out the cigarette in an ashtray on the mantle next to the closet, Ben pawed through the contents of the small space. He pushed aside clothes and bags on the floor, moved random containers on the shelf up above, until he found a shoebox that rattled when jostled. He struggled to keep the lid in place as he pulled the box toward him with one hand. The task would have been easier had he set the gun aside, but the weapon was now part of him. Primal instinct prevented him from letting go, as if he were a child with a new toy, or a very dangerous adult.

Ben set the box on the floor and removed the lid, revealing several small cartons of bullets. His heart started to race. *As long as there aren't too many of those things out there, I can make these last all night if I'm careful...* He closed the lid, put the dirty shoes on top of the box, and picked up the whole package with his free hand. Time to wake the woman on the couch in the dining room.

"...law enforcement member who keep track of the murder reports by the placing of markers on a map seem to indicate a general spreading from the extreme southeastern and states north and west. Our newsmen who have been on the telephone talking with officials of other cities have determined that none of this kind of mass murder has yet been reported west of the Mississippi river, except in the extreme southeastern portion of Texas. Similar killings have been reported around the Houston and Galveston areas but nothing like the..."

Ben returned to the dining room to find the woman sitting up on the couch. He'd hoped sleep would clear her mind, make her more responsive in a substantive way. But she seemed to be every bit as shell-shocked as when he'd arrived. *Great.*

"I found a gun and some bullets out there." Ben tried to sound upbeat. "Oh, and these." He held up the shoes. Nothing. *Well, she's going to need these if we leave, so she's putting them on whether she likes it or not...* Ben knelt down and gently placed the shoes on her feet. He decided that his best tactic would be to keep talking. Hopefully some optimistic conversation would draw her out. "This place is boarded up pretty solid now. We ought to be all right here for a while. We have a gun and bullets, food, and the radio. Sooner or later, someone's bound to come and get us out."

Her stone face threatened to bring his anger back, so he focused on loading the gun. The radio filled this brief pause.

"So again, we join with law enforcement agencies in urging you to seek shelter in a building. Lock the doors and windows securely."

Ben seized on this tiny opportunity for positivity. "Hey, that's us!" he said, indicating the boarded up windows and doors. "We're doing all right."

We're doing all right... Barbara stared at the man in front of her. *A gun... He has a gun...* She definitely didn't feel they were doing all right.

"Be cautious of any suspicious strangers, and keep tuned to your radio and television for survival instructions and further details of this continuing story."

Gun loaded, Ben was ready to move forward. The weapon felt good in his hand. The weight, the cold metal. The smooth wooden handle. He was finally ready to take on whatever those things threw at him.

But there was one last task he needed to deal with inside: that mess at the top of the stairs.

"Look, I don't know if you're hearing me, but I'm going upstairs now," Ben explained, patiently. "If anything should try to break in, I can hear it from up there, and I'll be down to take care of it." The woman's eyes narrowed slightly. What was she thinking? *Does she still not trust me?* "Everything is all right for now. I'll be back to reinforce the windows and doors later. But you'll be all right for now, okay?" No reaction. He reached out and touched her arm for emphasis. "Okay?" Nothing. He might as well have tried to communicate with the couch she was sitting on. *Fine...* Ben stood up and left the dining room.

Barbara didn't like that gun, didn't like the situation — and now, with the man climbing the stairs to the second floor, she didn't like being left alone. Her memory had come back to her. She understood where they were now (*the farmhouse...*), and she knew what waited for them beyond the boarded-up windows. (*Those men... Those men...*) The man upstairs was angry. And now he carried a gun. But somehow, she understood if she were ever going to see Johnny again, she had to stay inside. And she had to trust him.

She felt hot again, so she pulled off her coat, but she remained seated on the couch. She was just too scared to stand up.

"Civil defense officials in Cumberland have told newsmen that murder victims show evidence of having been partially devoured..."

THEY'RE EATING
THE FLESH OF THE PEOPLE
THEY MURDERED

Ben stopped one stair shy of the second floor. He averted his eyes from the mangled body in front of him, which led to his discovery of blood dripping from two large, shoulder-high splashes on the wall. *She must have been standing here when she was attacked...* Despite having seen the worst of this carnage earlier, Ben still felt his stomach turn at the sight. No amount of familiarity with the scene could dilute the sickening display of the total destruction of a woman's face. The anger, the fury with which her flesh had been ripped away was even more evident from this vantage point.

He hadn't known exactly what he was going to do with the body before he climbed the stairs, but a plan formed as he surveyed the gruesome scene. The woman had fallen on a rug, a runner covering the hardwood floor, so he would just drag the woman down the hall and lock the corpse in one of the bedrooms.

Ben leaned the shotgun against the wall as he stepped over the body onto the second-floor landing. This marked the first time he hadn't been in direct contact with the weapon since he'd taken possession of it downstairs. But his revulsion at the ugly aftermath of this vicious attack was something from which his newfound gun could not protect him.

Ben noticed the woman's feet were bare as he nudged them onto the runner. *Were those her shoes?* He shoved the thought from his mind as he folded the opposite end of the rug over what was left of the woman's head. Taking great care to avoid the sticky blood and gore, Ben gingerly took hold of the makeshift shroud and pulled toward the door at the far end of the hall. Avoiding glimpses of the mutilated corpse was almost impossible, so Ben half closed his eyes as he dragged the body to its final resting place.

In the dining room the radio continued to fill the air with unsettling information about the crisis unfolding in unprotected regions of the country. Barbara listened, finally able to absorb the terrible details.

"Consistent reports from witnesses to the effect that people who acted as though they were in a kind of trance were killing and eating their victims prompted authorities to examine the bodies of some of the victims."

Two images flashed into Barbara's mind as the announcer described the attackers' methods: the man in the cemetery trying to bite her, his fetid mouth open wide; and the moment after her brother's head hit the gravestone, when the man was on top of him, his mouth hidden near Johnny's neck. *Eating the victims?*

"Medical authorities in Cumberland have concluded that in all cases the killers are eating the flesh of the people they murdered."

Eating the flesh... The killers are eating the flesh... Her face went slack as the words reverberated in her mind, over and over again, hypnotically. *Eating the flesh... Killing and eating... Eating the flesh of the people they murdered...*

"*Repeating this latest bulletin just received moments ago from Cumberland, Maryland. Civil defense authorities have told newsmen that murdered victims show evidence of having been partially devoured by their murderers.*"

Partially devoured... Now her mind was creating images, gruesome images, of the man in the cemetery grinding his teeth into Johnny, tearing into his flesh, pulling bloody chunks of meat from her brother's neck. *Eating the flesh...* She felt faint again.

"*Medical examination of victims' bodies shows conclusively that the killers are eating the flesh of the people they kill.*"

The people they kill...

"*And so this incredible story becomes more ghastly with each report. It's difficult to imagine such a thing actually happening, but these are the reports we have been receiving and passing on to you, reports which have been verified as completely as is possible in this confused situation. It is happening. And it would appear that no one is safe from this mass murder.*"

Barbara was pulled from her grisly reverie by a noise emanating from... where? Near the hallway door? The sound, wood on wood, something being dragged, seemed to be coming from behind the oak door, which was now open and flush with the wall in the dining room. Barbara was confused. Where was that sound coming from? Inside the wall?

Fingers, then a hand snaked out from behind the door at chest height and curled around the edge. Barbara shook her head in disbelief. How could that be? There was no room behind that door...

Suddenly the door was pushed away from the wall. Before Barbara could process the fact there was a secret entrance into the room, two men burst through the doorway and ran toward her.

Barbara screamed.

UP FROM BELOW

Ben had just finished depositing the dead woman's body into the bedroom when a scream pierced the air. He bolted out into the hallway, grabbed the shotgun, and raced down the stairs.

He burst into the dining room, gun drawn. He found the woman fending off two men. *How did they get in?* The younger of the two held the woman by the shoulders. The older man brandished a tire iron, but he seemed to be avoiding contact with the woman, standing off to the side, watching nervously. As soon as Ben entered the room, the woman angrily pulled herself away from the two men and went back to the couch.

Both men's hands shot up. "Hold it! Don't shoot!" the younger man shouted. "We're from town!" Barely out of his teens, the young man carried no weapon, and was obviously not one of those things from the yard. In fact, he appeared to be harmless.

"The Butler county sheriff has verified that reports of murder victims being partially eaten by their slayers is true."

"A radio!" Short, heavyset, balding, with an injury to his scalp, the older man appeared to be more of a challenge. He brusquely pushed past Ben on his way into the den and knelt down in front of the radio.

Ben tried to relax. These men were obviously not here to do harm. He was about to question them when he saw the open basement door. "How long you guys been down there?" he asked angrily. "I could've used some help up here."

The bald man shrugged off the question. "That's the cellar. It's the safest place."

"You mean you didn't hear the racket we were making up here?" Ben demanded.

Harry Cooper did not care for this man's tone, and he certainly did not like being questioned. "How were we supposed to know what was going on? Could've been those things for all we knew." *Shut up and let me get some information from this news show…*

"That girl was screaming! Surely you must know what a girl screaming sounds like!" the man retorted sarcastically. "Those things don't make any noise. Anybody would know somebody needed help!"

Tom tried to bolster Mr. Cooper's point, even though he didn't completely agree. He didn't know who this man was, but a fight with a someone holding a gun was the last thing they needed now. "Look, it's kind of hard to hear what's going on from down there." He kept his tone even, nonconfrontational. What he didn't say was he'd heard the activity in the house, but Mr. Cooper had browbeaten him into staying put.

Cooper could sense he was caught, but pride wouldn't let him give in. He tried to reason with the man despite feeling the gesture was beneath him. "We thought we could hear screams, but for all we knew, that could have meant those things were in the house after her," he offered as an explanation.

"And you wouldn't come up and help?"

Tom tried to jump in again. "Well, if there were more…"

"The racket sounded like the place was being ripped apart," Cooper pointed out. "How were we supposed to know what was going on?" *Jesus Christ, who the hell does this guy think he is?* More than this man's tone and having his motives questioned by a stranger, Cooper hated being quizzed. *This guy thinks I'm lying?*

"Now wait a minute…" The answers didn't add up, and Ben wasn't going to let the bald guy get away with half-truths just because he was angry. Ben had faced angry men before, but there was something about this particular angry man he didn't like, something that made him want to needle the guy just a little bit more. He knew what the man was trying to say: He was scared, and he didn't want to risk opening the door. But he'd be damned if he was going to let this cowardly interloper and his friend justify their actions without some resistance. Besides, he'd worked hard to fortify the house, and if these men were going to stay here they were going to have to act like men and be forthright.

"You just got finished saying you couldn't hear it from down there. Now you say it sounded like the place was being ripped apart. It would be nice if you'd get your story straight, man." Ben took an amount of guilty pleasure from sticking it to this guy with his tone. And sure enough, the guy took the bait.

"All right, now you tell me!" Cooper stood up from his radio perch and placed himself toe-to-toe with his interrogator. *Questioning me like a goddamn lawyer…* Taller than him by a foot, holding a gun — Cooper didn't care. The guy didn't get to judge his choices just because he chose differently. "I'm not going to take that kind of a chance when we've got a safe place. We luck into a safe place, and you're telling us we've gotta risk our lives just because somebody might need help, huh?"

"Yeah. Something like that."

Once again, Tom tried to keep the peace. "All right, why don't we settle this…"

"Look, mister! We came up, okay? We're here." Cooper moved over to the cellar door. "Now I suggest we all go back downstairs before any of those things find out we're in here."

"They can't get in here," Ben replied dismissively. *Look around, man…*

Tom took in all the covered windows. "You got the whole place boarded up?"

"Yeah, most of it." The kid seemed okay, not a hothead like his buddy. Ben could tell they'd be able to work together up here. "All but a few spots upstairs. They won't be hard to fix."

"You're insane!" Cooper angrily gestured to the cellar door. "The cellar's the safest place!"

Ben was tired of the angry little man. "I'm telling you, they can't get in here."

"And I'm telling you, those things turned over our car!" Cooper shouted. "We were damned lucky to get away at all. Now you tell me those... those things..." Cooper tapped one of the planks that Ben had nailed across a window. "...can't get through this lousy pile of wood?"

Tom jumped in. "His wife and kid's downstairs. The kid's hurt."

A wife and hurt kid? Ben rethought his position. They already had one useless person up here, and keeping more weak people safe wasn't his first choice. But he needed to save face, at least for the moment. "Well, I still think we're better off up here," he stated matter-of-factly.

Tom turned to Mr. Cooper. He knew the man only from the time they'd spent in the basement together. But he understood men like Harry Cooper, men who needed to be in charge, men who operated from fear disguised as assertiveness and leadership. He knew the only way to get through to him was to negotiate. "We could strengthen everything up, Mr. Cooper."

Ben sensed an ally. "With all of us working, we could fix this place up in no time. We have everything we need up here." Again he felt like he was explaining the situation to a child, the difference being this Cooper guy was a petulant child who wanted everything his way.

Cooper couldn't believe his ears. "We can take all that stuff downstairs with us. Man, you're really crazy, you know that? You got a million windows up here." Cooper waved his hand in a sweeping gesture that took in the room and encompassed the entire house. "All these windows. You're gonna... You're gonna make 'em strong enough to keep these things out, huh?"

"I told you, those things don't have any strength," Ben countered. "I smashed three of them and pushed another one out the door!"

Jesus Christ, is this guy deaf? "Did you hear me when I told you they turned over our car?!"

"Oh hell, any good five men can do that."

"That's my point! Only there's not going to be five, or even ten. There's gonna be twenty, thirty, maybe a hundred of those things. And as soon as they know we're here, this place is gonna be crawling with them."

"Well, if there're that many, they'll probably get us wherever we are."

Normally Cooper wouldn't have kept trying to convince someone to do something his way. Normally this guy could go to Hell. But the guy had a gun, and Cooper wanted it. If not in his own hands, then at least nearby. "Look, the cellar. The cellar." Cooper pointed to the crudely cut door. "There's only one door, right? Just one door. That's all we have to protect. Tom and I fixed it so it locks and boards from the inside. But up here, all these windows, why, we'd never know where they were gonna hit us next."

"You got a point, Mr. Cooper. But down in the cellar, there's no place to run to." Tom tried to appeal to Cooper's sense of logic. "I mean, if they did get in, there'd be no back exit. We'd be done for."

Cooper waved him off and moved over to the woman on the couch. He realized she hadn't spoken a word since they'd emerged from the cellar. *What's wrong with her?*

Tom pressed on. "We can get out of here if we have to. And we got windows to see what's going on outside. But down there, with no windows — if a rescue party did come, we wouldn't even know it."

"But the cellar is the strongest place."

"The cellar is a death trap." Ben was finished arguing with this Cooper guy.

But Tom felt he could convince him so he kept on. "I don't know, Mr. Cooper. I think he's right." Tom turned to Ben. "You know how many's out there?"

"I don't know, I figure maybe six or seven."

Cooper didn't care if there were five or a thousand of those things outside. There would be more, and soon. "Look, you two can do whatever you like. I'm going back down to the cellar and you better decide, 'cause I'm gonna board up that door, and I'm not gonna unlock it again no matter what happens."

"Now wait a minute, Mr. Cooper…"

"No, I'm not gonna wait! I've made my decision, now you make yours!"

"Now wait a minute! Let's think about this." Tom couldn't believe Mr. Cooper would actually lock them out, but he wasn't happy with the idea he might get trapped upstairs. Cooper had to listen to logic. "We can make it to the cellar if we have to. And if we do decide to stay down there, we'll need some things from up here. So let's at least consider this a while." Tom's forceful retort quieted Cooper momentarily. The older man studied his hands in silence.

"If you box yourself in the cellar and those things get in the house, you've had it." Ben wanted that cellar as an option, regardless of whether or not he felt the space was safer than upstairs. *Can't let that stubborn jackass lock that door… Have to convince him…* "At least up here, you have a fighting chance."

Tom peered out the window. The group of ghouls, now joined by more women and a man in a hospital gown, tottered around the truck. "Yeah, looks like about eight or ten of them now."

"That's more than there were. There're a lot out back, too." Ben headed toward the kitchen to check on what he expected to be a growing crowd in the backyard. But what he didn't expect were the two mangled hands that burst through the space between the boards on the window and grabbed him.

THEY GATHER

Tom raced into the kitchen as Ben tried to free himself from the hands attacking him through the window. The young man searched for a weapon and grabbed the first ones he found: the pieces of kindling still sitting on the cupboard shelf.

Ben tried to point the shotgun at the ghouls outside, but they held him too close to the window, leaving him no room to maneuver. He pushed himself backward off the wall, yanking his clothing from the attackers' hands. Now that he had room to properly aim the gun, Ben shoved the barrel through the space between the boards. Two hands grabbed the business end of the shotgun and tried to pull the weapon out the window. Ben hesitated to pull the trigger. His instinct was to make every bullet count, and if he wasn't careful the shot might fly off harmlessly into the distance.

Tom beat at yet another greedy hand grabbing through the window. Despite the violence of their attack, the ghouls were eerily quiet. Not a word. Not a moan. The silence unnerved Tom, as did the fact he thought he recognized the man outside. He held back for the first blow, the second, fighting not only the ghoul but his own instinctive resistance against harming someone he knew. But the hand did not relent. He struck the hand again, hard, then harder, over and over, the force of the blows rising with his anger. *Stay back*! The fingers bent, folded, broke off as Tom assaulted them with the wood. Yet despite the cracked bones and torn flesh, the creature on the other end refused to retreat. Tom used all of his strength for one last strike. The kindling severed the hand at the wrist. The strangely bloodless stump retreated from the window.

Ben pulled the gun back, repositioned the barrel through the wooden barricade, and pulled the trigger. *Bam!*

The attacker staggered backward as the bullet traveled in through his chest and out his lower back. But the creature retreated not from injury, but rather the physical force of the shot. Apparently uninjured, or unconcerned, he launched himself at the window again.

"Harry? Harry, what's happening?" A woman's voice floated up from the cellar.

Cooper, who'd been watching Ben and Tom from a safe distance, called back. "It's all right!" But he didn't believe that, not for one second. *That thing just took a bullet, and it's still standing!*

Ben fired again, and another hole appeared in the creature's torso. And again he staggered back to the window, undaunted. Ben took a breath and carefully aimed the shotgun's sight directly at the ghoul's forehead.

"Now take it…" He pulled the trigger. A quarter-sized hole appeared in the creature's forehead as brains, blood, and bone exploded out the back of his skull. The ghoul fell to the ground, motionless, his finally dead eyes open wide.

INTERMISSION

Edgar was in his shirtsleeves, oblivious to the fact the temperature had dropped to almost 50 degrees once the sun set. Earlier in the day he'd been inside the house with his wife. Now she was upstairs wrapped in a blanket, and he was wandering outside in the yard. He didn't have any visible injuries, but the tilt of his head suggested something was very wrong with his neck. If there was any pain, Edgar seemed unfazed.

Others, two-dozen or more, joined Edgar outside his home. Some were neighbors he'd known well. Some were merely passing acquaintances. Some were complete strangers. Some were drawn to the house because of the sounds that emanated from within. Some were drawn to the light, which now served as a kind of beacon. And some followed Ben's and the Coopers' vehicles, albeit at a great distance. Instinct kept them on the road until they were close enough to hear the sounds, or to see the lights.

Some had just been wandering, directionless, until they crossed paths with others, at which point a herd mentality took over and a direction silently agreed upon.

There was Joe, a middle-aged man who didn't live in the area, but who spent a night or two each month in a local motel as he passed through on business. Despite the cold, Joe was wearing just his boxers. He sported a ragged wound — the flesh torn from his shoulder down to his heart appeared to have been ripped by some kind of crude knife, or maybe an axe. Yet here he was, on his feet, circling the farmhouse.

The woman in the plain housedress was Susan — a wife, mother of three boys, bookkeeper at a dentist's office one town over. She'd rushed home two days ago after being called by her sons' school. One of the boys had gotten a nasty bite during a fight on the playground, and an infection seemed to be spreading fast. The boy got sicker and sicker, and finally became violent. And now she'd arrived at the farmhouse after walking for almost a full day.

The old man in the hospital gown was Silas Greene, the local pharmacist. Silas was in the middle of a routine physical yesterday when an angry patient from the E.R. burst into the exam room and attacked him. The deep gashes on his face and neck suggested he'd lost that fight.

The skin on Marilyn's face was bloated and mottled after lying face down in a shallow pool of water for two days, after which she'd gotten up and walked out of her house. She'd followed the Coopers' car to this isolated area, and was finally approaching Edgar's home. As she passed a tree near the edge of the property, Marilyn spotted a centipede crawling in and out of the crags of bark. She pulled the arthropod from the tree, regarded it for a moment, then shoved the wriggling creature into her mouth and chewed.

The nude woman whom Ben had glimpsed earlier was Jennifer Donahue, a waitress from Beekman's Diner. Jennifer hadn't been to work in several days, and the manager had been on the verge of calling the sheriff on the day the diner was attacked. Were she close enough for Ben, Cooper, or any of the other current occupants of the farmhouse to notice the plastic bracelet on her wrist, they could have read:

PRIMROSE COUNTY MORGUE
NAME: JENNIFER DONAHUE
D.O.D.: 9-14-68
CAUSE OF DEATH: ASPHYXIATION

There were more of them, many more, wandering the countryside. Some would end up at Edgar's farmhouse. Some would find themselves miles away from their own homes. They were from different backgrounds, social groups. Lower class, middle class, even the wealthiest. They were different ages and races and religious affiliations.

But they all had one thing in common...

UP OR DOWN

Dammit!

Ben backed away from the kitchen window, panicked. Those things just shoved their hands through the glass as if the panes weren't there, then reached through the spaces between the boards. He'd thought he'd done a thorough job barricading the house, but he'd forgotten about the ghouls' willingness to injure themselves. *Remember the diner, dammit!* The spaces between the boards were big enough to reach through, which meant they were big enough for those things to grab onto the planks and pull them down. Well, now they needed to rethink how they protected themselves, starting with the windows.

"We've gotta fix these boards!" He meant the three of them, but he already knew Cooper's response.

"You're crazy!" Once again Cooper was amazed at what an idiot this guy was. "Those things are gonna be at every window and door in this place! We've got to get down into the cellar!"

Ben was willing to look past the fact this coward refused to help when those things reached through the window, but he'd be damned if he was going let Cooper shove him around when their lives depended on the choices they were making. "Go down into your damn cellar and get out of here!" he shouted at the little man.

Tom took a step back into the kitchen doorway, hesitant to get between the two arguing men. This could get ugly, especially with a gun involved.

And Cooper wanted that gun. He needed to either get the weapon out of this moron's hands (doubtful, at least at the moment) or get the moron down into the cellar with them (tough, but possible). The conversation couldn't end now. *How do I get him downstairs? The girl!* The worthless girl on the couch might be of some use after all. "I'm... I'm taking the girl with me." He reached down to pull the woman off the couch.

Barbara looked up at the angry man. Did he mean her?

"You leave her here!" Ben commanded. Cooper stopped, surprised at the intensity in the man's voice. Ben didn't have any particular attachment to the woman, but he wasn't going to let Cooper get her killed. "Keep your hands off her, and everything else that's up here, too," he continued. "Because if I stay up here, I'm fighting for everything up here. And the radio and the food is part of what I'm fighting for!" *That ought to shut him up.* "Now if you're going down in the cellar, get!"

Cooper turned to Tom, incredulous. *No food?* "The man's insane. He's insane." He was desperate to get Tom on his side. "We've... We've got to have food down there. We've got a right."

"This your house?" Ben asked.

What the hell did that matter? "We've got a right!"

Ben turned to the young man. He was done with this foolishness. "You going down there with him?"

Tom was torn. "Well, I..."

"Yes or no?" Ben barked. "This is your last chance. No beating around the bush."

Tom couldn't answer. His mind raced as he frantically weighed his options.

Cooper sensed he'd lost the argument, but the thought of his child in danger compelled him to press on. *I gotta get this guy to listen to reason.* "Listen, I got a kid down there," he said, backing off his machismo. Despite being a blowhard, Cooper truly loved his daughter. He was willing to eat some crow and end the chest thumping if making this guy feel like he was the big boss meant some sort of compromise. "She can't possibly... I couldn't bring her up here. She can't possibly take all the racket from those things smashing through the windows."

Ben was having none of it. "Well, you're her father. If you're stupid enough to go die in that trap, that's your business. However, I am not stupid enough to follow you." And maybe an extra twist of the knife, just because this guy was such a pain in the ass. "It is tough for the kid that her old man is so stupid," Ben casually lobbed at Cooper. "Now, get the hell down in the cellar. You can be the boss down there. I'm boss up here."

Cooper was so furious at this halfwit's monologue his vision blurred. How dare he drag his daughter into this? "You bastards!" Ben turned his back on Cooper and focused his attention on fortifying the windows. "You know, I won't open this door again. I mean it."

"Mr. Cooper, with your help we can..."

Cooper waved Tom off. "With my help." *Yeah, right...*

"Let him go, man." Ben was completely exasperated with this guy. "His mind is made up. Just let him go."

Steaming, Cooper turned and pushed open the door to the cellar. *Let that stubborn idiot kill himself...*

Tom's mouth dropped open in shock. He couldn't believe the two men couldn't — or wouldn't — come to an agreement on what seemed to be a very simple compromise. Was Mr. Cooper really going to lock that door?

"Wait a minute." Tom pulled Cooper out of the doorway and leaned into the cellar stairway. "Judy?" he called down. "Come on up here, honey."

A pretty girl about Tom's age cautiously emerged from the cellar. She'd heard the argument between the men, and even though she hadn't been able to make out what they were saying, she was apprehensive about leaving the safe space downstairs. As soon as she saw the tall man with a gun and the catatonic woman on the couch, she stopped.

"You're gonna let them get her too, huh?" Cooper was done with the lot of them. After all he'd done to keep these two kids safe, they were going to throw it all away on this hothead upstairs.

"It's all right, honey." Tom gave Judy a gentle, reassuring push toward the couch. "Go ahead." Judy was confused. *Why are we leaving the cellar?* She perched on the arm of the sofa, not daring to get too close to the strange woman.

A girlfriend? How many people do they have down there? Ben watched the new arrival intently. Was she going to be another burden up here, like the woman on the couch? She seemed scared, but at least she was aware of her surroundings. *Just carry your weight, that's all I ask...*

Without another word, Cooper exited the dining room into the basement stairwell. Once inside he shut the door, turned the lock, then picked up the two-by-four leaning against the wall and slid the beam into the braces on either side of the doorframe. *They'll see...*

As soon as the barricade was in place, Cooper could hear Tom pleading from the dining room. "If we stick together, man, we can fix it up real good," Tom begged. "There's lots of places we can run to up here." *Yeah, right, kid.*

In the dining room, Tom waited for an answer. Silence. One more try. "Mr. Cooper? We'd all be a lot better off if all three of us were working together." Nothing. Silence downstairs and upstairs. Without the argument filling the room, the house was suddenly eerily quiet.

Judy wasn't sure what to do about the woman on the couch. Was she hurt? Why was she acting like nothing was happening? Was she with the man with the gun? Just as Judy was about to reach out and try to establish some kind of contact, the man with the gun knelt down in front of the woman.

"Hey. Hey, kid." Ben kept his tone light, upbeat, as if to say, *We're good now! No need to worry!* He looked into her eyes, but she was still somewhere else. Shaking his head in resignation, Ben pulled the pack of smokes out of his pocket. As he shook a cigarette out of the pack, he turned to the young couple.

"He's wrong, you know." They studied him and said nothing as he lit his cigarette. "I'm not boxing myself in down there."

THE SAFEST PLACE

Cooper descended the wooden staircase into the cellar. He looked back up toward the door, reassuring himself the one entrance to their sanctuary was indeed secure. None of those things would be getting down here. Neither would Tom nor the others, but that was their problem.

"Well, we're safe now," he said in a manner that suggested he was trying to convince himself. "It's boarded up tight."

The cellar was a rudimentary affair. One room, four stark cement walls, a sturdy wooden support pillar in the center of the space. Around the perimeter were a washer and dryer, a large utility sink, and mismatched shelves filled with random junk accumulated by a family over several decades. Two bare light bulbs hung from the ceiling, their low-watt yellow light unable to penetrate the deeper recesses of the dank, subterranean hideout. The floor was mortarless brick laid over hard-packed earth, which meant a thick layer of dust and grime was always present. The lack of ventilation combined with the moisture from the washing machine guaranteed the air was stale, wet, and heavy.

In the middle of the room, a semi-conscious eleven-year-old girl lay on a makeshift table assembled from two sawhorses and an old door. Covered with a coat, head resting on a folded blanket, the girl's breath was deliberate, labored. Perspiration beaded on her forehead. A bloody injury on her arm had been covered with an improvised bandage made from torn fabric.

Sitting on a broken chair next to the table was a middle-aged woman — attractive with a hard edge, brunette hair piled on top of her head, dressed comfortably for travel. Even as the woman spoke to Cooper, she stared at the young girl in front of her, desperate for any sign the child's condition was improving.

"What about Tom and Judy?"

"They wanna stay up there, let 'em," Cooper replied, tossing the tire iron aside for emphasis, the clang of metal on the brick floor a jarring punctuation to his ire. The woman didn't reply, her silence ensuring Cooper knew she'd purposefully not responded. She focused on the girl, not looking up at Cooper as he paced around their small cell. A casual observer of this scene would assume not only were they married, but this was not an unusual dynamic in their relationship.

"There are two other people up there," Cooper continued, "A man and a girl." There was a tinge of guilt in his voice. Now that the fireworks had subsided and his sparring partner was locked out of the room, he felt slightly uncomfortable with the way the situation played out upstairs. *If he just would've listened to reason...* He searched his pockets for his cigarettes.

"We heard the screaming," his wife replied. A gentle jab with a soft knife. *Of course there are people upstairs, Harry...*

"Yeah, but I didn't know who they were." Cooper's pack of cigarettes came up empty. *Dammit.* "And I wasn't about to take any unnecessary chances."

"Of course not, Harry." A casual twist of the blade. Cooper glared at his wife, his rage at the asinine implication of her tone rising by the millisecond. *Who the hell does she think I'm protecting down here? Don't say it. Don't. Say. It.* Instead of taking his anger out on her verbally or physically — and he was tempted by both options — he channeled his rage into the fist that held the empty cigarette pack. He crumpled the thin cardboard, took a step away from the table, and hurled the crushed container to the ground. His wife pointedly failed to react to his tantrum, even as he spun around and glared at her again as if she had. She kept her face pointed toward their daughter and watched him out of the corner of her eye, knowing her lack of response would anger him even more.

Cooper wasn't ready to let her accusatory subtext go — but then he absorbed the sight of his daughter on the cot, injured and so ill. The tension left his body. He reached down and caressed his daughter's forehead.

"Is she all right?"

"I don't know what it is. She feels warm. Maybe it's shock." No subtext this time; her tone was soft. She was an expert at this game. She knew when to push Harry to the brink, and when to retreat. But more importantly, her daughter was unconscious on a slab of wood in the cellar of a stranger's house. Her concern for her little girl's well being left her little energy or desire to engage in an argument for sport.

"Where'd you get the bandage?"

"Some laundry in a basket. I tore a sheet."

Cooper still needed that cigarette, so he opened his wife's purse and rummaged around until he found her pack of lights. Not his first choice, but neither was being locked in a cellar. He pulled out a smoke and placed it between his lips, then he dug around until he located a book of matches. He lit the cigarette, pulled a hefty amount of nicotine into his lungs, and paused for a moment to consider their situation.

"Let them stay upstairs. Let them," he said magnanimously, as if granting permission to Tom, Judy, and the rest of the upstairs contingent. "Too many ways those monsters can get in up there. We'll see who's right." He was convincing himself now, his confidence bolstered by an abundance of nicotine and the absence of an opposing argument. "We'll see, when they come begging me to let them in down here."

"That's important, isn't it?" She couldn't help herself. The knife was back out.

"What?"

"To be right. Everybody else to be wrong." Her husband was The Great Scorekeeper, he never forgot a slight, opposing view, or cross word.

Jesus Christ, are we going to go through this again? "What do you mean by that?"

She waved him off and he went back to pacing, satisfied he'd shut her up. This was, of course, a convenient fiction — she'd been married to him long enough to know how to play him like a pinball machine. She shut up when she was ready to shut up. And she was smart enough to know escalating an argument while they were trapped in a cellar was a losing game.

"Does anyone up there know why we're being attacked?"

Cooper sat down on the on the foot of the table, his exhaustion catching up with him. "Whatever it is, it isn't just happening here. It's some kind of mass murder. It's going on everywhere. The radio said to stay inside..."

"Radio?" Her expression instantly transformed to one of disbelief.

"The radio, upstairs. I heard the news bulletin..."

Cooper's wife slowly rose from her seat, boring holes through him with her eyes. "There's a radio upstairs, and you boarded us in down here?"

"I know what I'm doing!"

"What did it say?" Her voice drilled into him like an auger.

"Nothing!" Cooper waved his hands dismissively. "Nothing. They don't know anything yet." The pure fury in his wife's expression drove him from his seat. He stood up and started pacing, facing away from her as he explained what he'd heard. "The... There's mass murder everywhere, and people are supposed to look for a safe place to hide." He gestured to their surroundings as the perfect example of exactly that.

"Take the boards off that door." She rarely demanded anything from him, but this was not a request.

Cooper spun around to face her. "We are staying down here, Helen!"

"Harry, that radio is at least some kind of communication," she coaxed. "If the authorities know what's happening, well, they'll send people for us, or they'll tell us what to do!" Her panic at the possibility of losing an opportunity for rescue caused Helen to lose control of her voice. Angry tears welled up around the edges of her words. "How are we going to know what's going on, if we lock ourselves in this dungeon?"

Cooper threw down his cigarette and once again angrily turned to face her, but this time he wasn't arguing. He was threatening. *Shut. Up.*

And Helen did. A smart woman, she knew a fight wasn't the way out of this cellar, so she averted her eyes and sat down. This was a tactic, not deference.

Glowering, Cooper stalked over to the bottom of the stairs, the matter settled in his mind. Helen, however, was not finished. Circumstances had changed, and now she needed to act on her daughter's behalf rather than let her husband bully his way through this crisis. One deep breath, and then a plain statement of fact.

"We may not enjoy living together... but dying together isn't going to solve anything." There it was. The truth. The acknowledgment of their situation, out loud. The beginning of the end of their marriage if they ever escaped this basement. But if speaking the truth saved their daughter... "Those people aren't our enemies."

"Mr. Cooper!" Tom's voice drifted into the cellar from behind the barred door. "Mr. Cooper? Ben found a television set upstairs."

Helen's face lit up. She popped up from her chair and darted over to Cooper. Squeezing his arms she looked directly into his eyes with a smile. *Truce?* "Let's go up," she implored. Cooper kept his poker face. He wanted to go up, was desperate to watch a news broadcast, but just couldn't bring himself to verbally agree. Helen forged ahead, sliding past her husband so she could talk to Tom.

"Tom?" she called up.

"Yes?"

"If Judy would come downstairs for a few minutes, Harry and I could come upstairs."

"Okay, yeah. Right away."

Cooper turned away from Helen, but she knew his silence was his consent.

They would go upstairs.

On the other side of the door Tom turned to Judy. "Will you do it?"

"Do I have to?" Judy hated being trapped in that basement, and she hated the idea of being separated from Tom even more. What if something happened to him?

"Look, honey, nothing's gonna get done with them down there and us up here." Tom squeezed Judy's shoulder affectionately for emphasis. "Do this. For me."

Judy looked down and shrugged. "Okay..." Not that she felt she truly had a choice.

Tom called back to Cooper. "Okay, open up."

At the top of the cellar stairs, Cooper slid the two-by-four out of the braces and set the beam aside. He pulled open the door, which brought him face to face with Judy. She slid by him awkwardly, trying to avoid both eye and physical contact. She wasn't a good enough actress to hide her dislike for Cooper, and that drove him crazy. What in the name of God had he done to her? Protect her? Keep her safe? Well, she didn't have to like him. He was going to keep her safe until help arrived, and then she'd be grateful.

As Judy descended the stairs she saw Helen standing over the little girl, holding her hand and caressing her arm. *Poor woman, married to that awful man, trapped here with a sick daughter.* She couldn't imagine spending the rest of her life with Mr. Cooper — or worse, having him as her dad. But as bad as she felt for Helen, she didn't want to be stuck down here babysitting.

"I'll take good care of her, Helen."

"She's all I have." Despite the battle she'd just fought with her husband, Helen couldn't bear to leave her child's side. And now, her daughter's whole body felt hot to the touch.

Is she getting worse?

"Why don't you go upstairs now?" Judy gently prodded. Helen nodded grimly, then turned and headed up the stairs.

NEGOTIATED TRUCE

Cooper emerged from the cellar into the dining room. He brushed past Tom and stalked around the room surveying the unsatisfactory work on the windows.

Helen followed her husband up the stairs, but stopped short at the sight of the blonde on the couch. The woman was half sitting, half prone across the cushions, her face inches from the doily that covered the armrest. She traced the crocheted ridges with her finger, fixated on the pattern.

Tom noticed Helen's confusion. "Her brother was killed," he explained.

Helen stared at the girl, transfixed by the physical manifestation of a broken mind. *What must she have seen?* She thought of her daughter and the attack on the car, those things grabbing at her, biting her. When they got out of here — and Helen was confident they would — what trauma would her little girl carry with her? Would she, too, be broken?

"Hey, give me a hand with this thing." A voice from upstairs Helen didn't recognize.

"I gotta go help Ben with the television." Tom left the room and trotted up the stairs.

Cooper finished his dining-room inspection and exited into the den, leaving his wife alone with the stranger on the couch.

Helen's maternal instincts kicked in and she took a tentative step toward the silent woman, but then she reconsidered and retreated. Despite the calm exterior, she had no idea what was transpiring in the woman's mind, so she decided just to observe for the time being.

She sat down on one of the wooden dining chairs facing the couch. She looked around, taking in the current condition of the room. They hadn't spent much time up here before barricading themselves in the cellar, but windows boarded up with table tops, wood scraps, and ironing boards transformed this room into a fortress.

The woman on the couch was disturbed neither by Helen's presence nor the noise from upstairs. Helen felt a mixture of pity and annoyance as she watched this mute stranger, lost in her reverie. *Why did they leave me alone with her? And what the hell is Harry doing?*

Helen pulled a backup pack of cigarettes out of her coat pocket, the one she kept hidden because Harry was forever running out of his own and raiding her purse, then complaining she only had lights. She put a cigarette to her lips and struck a match.

Barbara's attention was instantly drawn to the flame. Her eyes followed the tiny fire as the woman on the chair raised the match to the cigarette. *He lit that man on fire... He pushed that man out the door and lit him on fire...* Still silent, her expression buckled into one of confusion and fear.

Helen sensed a change and looked up from lighting her cigarette. The silent woman watched her from the couch, finally acknowledging her presence with an unblinking, panicked stare, obviously scared of something.

"Don't be afraid of me," Helen said, gently. "I'm Helen Cooper." Then she added, "Harry's wife," on the very slim chance he'd made a positive impression on the woman during his first trip upstairs. The woman's expression only intensified, and Helen realized she was staring at the lit match. She shook the flame out with the slightest of movements, worried she might spook the girl if she moved too quickly. Success, of a sort. The girl relaxed and returned her attention to the doily on the couch arm.

Cooper stormed back in from the den. "This place is ridiculous!" He marched over to the window and shook one of the boards, which wiggled easily in his hand. "Look at this. There's a million weak spots up here." He spied Helen's cigarettes and snatched the pack out of her hand. "Give me one of those." *Goddamn lights…*

Helen just shook her head ruefully rather than chastise him because she knew how to pick her battles. *Of course it's a light, you moron…* What bothered her more was her husband's expression as he stared at the woman on the couch, the woman so traumatized she was mute and obviously having some kind of mental breakdown. He regarded her angrily, as if she were a piece of furniture that was out of place.

"Her brother was killed," Helen pointedly informed her husband.

He drew on the cigarette and nodded, jaw clenched, signaling that yes, he'd taken this information in, but whatever he felt about the situation didn't include sympathy. *Tough break, but not my problem…*

"And they talk about these windows," Cooper continued, addressing the *real* problem of the moment. "I can't see a damned thing." He paced around the room, making a show of not being able to see past the boards. "There could be fifteen million of those things out there. That's how much good these windows are."

Helen rolled her eyes and clenched her fists in frustration. Her husband, who as usual had all the advice and opinions in the world, wasn't lifting a finger, also as usual. He fancied himself an assessor, a person who would find the flaws. Fixing those flaws was a problem for those who followed orders, a group that did not include him.

While Cooper paced, he made a mental checklist of the shortcomings of everything and everyone in this damned house.

His wife frequently accused him of keeping score, but he preferred to see his vigilance as keeping *track*. Someone had to keep track.

His to-and-fro put Helen on edge, and she couldn't hold her tongue any longer. "Why don't you do something to help somebody?" She was practically shouting at him, but he continued to ignore her.

Tom and Ben returned to the dining room, their arrival pulling the Coopers away from their brewing spat. Tom led, walking backwards as they struggled to hold the large television set between them.

"Here, I have it," Ben said as he adjusted his grip. "Drag a couple of those chairs together." He leaned back and took the full weight of the set in his arms, allowing Tom to grab two dining chairs. Ben indicated a spot along the wall with his head. "There's a socket over here."

The girl's attention was pulled from the doily to the two men arranging the television on the chairs. Cooper took the opportunity to try to strengthen the team's weak link. He moved closer to the aggravatingly silent woman and wagged his finger at her. "Now, you'd better watch this and try to understand what's going on," he lectured sternly. She recoiled from his tone and gesture. Ben shot him a look from across the room. Cooper shrugged angrily. "I don't want anyone's life on my hands," he shouted in response.

"Is there anything I can do to help?" Helen asked, trying to insert herself between the two men before her husband managed to magically transform the conversation into a fight.

Ben ignored her. He'd be damned if this dunce was going to start running the show now that he had deigned to come up from his deathtrap. "I don't want to hear any more from you, mister!" he shouted. "If you stay up here, you take orders from me! And that includes leaving the girl alone!"

Before Cooper could respond, Tom shushed them all.

"It's on! It's on!"

THE TELEVISION

The image on the black-and-white television faded in as the set warmed up. A bespectacled news anchor spoke directly to the camera, but the weak signal, barely captured by the antennae, was not enough to transmit sound. Thankfully, the holes in the poor reception were filled in by the anchor's expression — grave concern, uncertainty, confusion. He was jacketless, sporting a wrinkled button-down shirt and a loosened tie. He looked as if he'd been on camera for more than a few hours and had abandoned formality at some point along the way. The complete picture suggested whatever was happening outside the studio was unexpected and unsettling.

"There's no sound," Cooper complained, ignoring the fact Tom was still trying to tune in the broadcast. "Play with the rabbit ears," he directed. Ben stepped in, moved Tom aside, and adjusted the antennae. Finally the picture locked into place and the voice of the anchor could be heard.

"Reports, incredible as they seem, are not the results of mass hysteria."

"'Mass hysteria,'" Cooper snorted. "What do they think, we're imagining all this?"

Jesus Christ, would you just... "Shut up!" Ben waved Cooper off. Chastened, Cooper sat on the couch. Ben and Tom settled in, and Helen pulled her chair closer to the set.

"*...in all parts of the country. The wave of murder which is sweeping the eastern third of the nation is being committed by creatures who feast upon the flesh of their victims.*"

Behind the news anchor, more reporters, researchers, and producers could be seen. They, too, had shed their jackets and rolled up their sleeves. They answered phones, scribbled notes, ran back and forth, gathered the disturbing information, and edited the most reliable reports for consumption by viewers. They were professionals, familiar with handling breaking news — but the reports coming in strained credulity even for the most experienced staffers.

"*First eyewitness accounts of this grisly development came from people who were understandably frightened and almost incoherent. Officials and newsmen at first discounted those eyewitness descriptions as being beyond belief.*"

Although he'd occupied the news desk for many years, the anchor wasn't used to speaking extemporaneously for such an extended period of time, and certainly not about a situation as unfathomable as the one in which he now found himself. His personal feelings began to creep into his reporting, and he reminded himself to stick to the verifiable facts.

"*However, the reports persisted. Medical examinations of some of the victims bore out the fact that they had been partially devoured.*"

Devoured. Helen shuddered. One of those things had bitten her daughter. Did he really intend to... eat her?

The anchor reacted to a signal off camera.

"I think we have some late word just arriving, and we interrupt to bring this to you."

He reached back and was handed a sheaf of papers.

"This is the latest disclosure in a report from National Civil Defense headquarters in Washington. It has been established that persons who have recently died have been returning to life and committing acts of murder. A widespread investigation of reports from funeral homes, morgues, and hospitals has concluded that the unburied dead are coming back to life and seeking human victims."

The news anchor set the report down and once again spoke directly to the audience, sounding less like a newsman and more like a worried citizen.

"It's hard for us here to believe what we're reporting to you, but it does seem to be a fact."

The five people sitting in front of the television in the abandoned farmhouse could now put aside all other theories, speculation, and educated guesses. They had their answer. Dead people were coming back to life. Corpses, from anywhere, everywhere, were rising up and butchering the living. Feasting on their flesh. Attacking and devouring them — and, presumably, creating more of their kind. An unbelievable ongoing assault, something you'd read in a pulp novel or see in a cheap B-movie, almost impossible to reconcile with reality. And yet...

The collective dread in the dining room was tangible, filling the dining room like warm water as Ben, Cooper, Helen, Tom, and Barbara digested the information disseminated by the news broadcast.

The news anchor swallowed hard, composed himself, and continued with his report.

"When this emergency first began, radio and television was advising people to stay inside, behind locked doors, for safety. Well, that situation has now changed."

That situation has now changed. The finality of that statement, and the gravity with which it was delivered, chilled the occupants of the dining room. Ben, Cooper, Tom, and Helen all understood. Upstairs or downstairs, the point was moot. They had to leave the house.

"We're able to report a definite course of action for you. Civil defense machinery has been organized to provide rescue stations with food, shelter, medical treatment, and protection by armed National Guardsmen. Stay tuned to the broadcasting stations in your local area for this list of rescue stations. This list will be repeated throughout our news coverage. Look for the name of the rescue station nearest you, and make your way to that location as soon as possible..."

As the news anchor spoke, names of towns and corresponding emergency shelters appeared at the bottom of the screen. *Youngstown, Township Municipal Hospital. Sharon, Central Fire Department. Mercer, Municipal Building...*

Ben jumped on the anchor's instructions. *Makes sense... If we wait any longer more of those things will probably get in...* "So we have that truck. If we can get some gas, we can get outta here!"

Tom chimed in. "There's a pump out by the shed."

"I know. That's why I pulled in here. But it's locked."

"An emergency meeting was called this afternoon by the President. Since convening, this conference of the Presidential cabinet, The FBI, the Joint Chiefs of Staff, the CIA has not

produced any public information. Why are space experts being consulted about an earthbound emergency?"

The question added another layer of inconceivability to an already impossible-to-believe situation. The occupants of the dining room exchanged skeptical looks. *Outer space?*

"So far, all the betting on the answer to that question centers on the recent Explorer satellite shot to Venus. That satellite, you recall, started back to Earth, but never got here. That's the space vehicle which orbited Venus and then was purposely destroyed by NASA, when scientists discovered it was carrying a mysterious, high-level radiation with it. Could that radiation be somehow responsible for the wholesale murders we're now suffering? Newsman Don Quinn in Washington has posed those questions..."

Ben was ready to go. "It's obvious. Our best move is to try to get out of here."

Cooper wanted to get out of there as much as anyone, but he wasn't going to just run out of the house without a plan. "How're you gonna get over to that pump?"

Ben didn't respond. He knew they could, he just needed to work out the details...

But then Tom pointed excitedly at the television. "Look!"

WASHINGTON, D.C.

The news camera followed a small crowd of men as they exited a cold, anonymous federal building and made their way toward the street. At the center of the group were three men, all very different, yet obviously united in some way. As they strode away from the building, the shaky video feed revealed they were being chased not only by the cameraman but three reporters and a soundman as well.

Of the three pursued men, a military man in a general's uniform seemed to be the leader. He was flanked on his left by a dark-haired, bearded man holding a briefcase, and on his right by a clean-shaven man in a trench coat.

Much like the general, one of the newsmen seemed to be the leader of his predatory pack of journalists. Don Quinn, a beat reporter for the D.C. area, had a large frame and long hair that made him stand out in this briskly moving congregation, as did the nontraditional large-print houndstooth jacket he wore over a dark turtleneck. As the general and his colleagues walked toward a military sedan parked at the curb, Quinn took point while the others scrambled, desperately repositioning their microphones at the moving targets.

"You're coming from a meeting regarding the explosion of the Venus probe, is that right?" Quinn aimed his mic at the general.

"Yes, yes, that was the subject of the meeting."

"Do you feel there is a connection between this and the phenomenon...?"

The bearded man interrupted, cutting off what he assumed would be the general's denial. "There's a definite connection. A definite connection."

Quinn pushed harder. "In other words, you feel that the radiation on the Venus probe is enough to cause these mutations?"

"It was a very high degree of radiation," the bearded man replied, implying an affirmative response to the reporter's question.

"Well, just a minute," the general jumped in, distancing himself from the bearded man's revelation. "I'm not sure that that's certain at all. I don't think that has been..."

"It's the only logical explanation that we have at this time," the clean-shaven man interjected. Rattled by the unexpected attention from the reporters, he reflexively spoke the truth, anticipating his statement would end the conversation.

But on the contrary, this was exactly the fuel Quinn needed to press on. Sensing a division of opinion among the men, he decided to drive in a wedge between them. "In other words, it is the military's viewpoint that this... the radiation is not the cause of the mutation." He pointed his microphone at the general.

"I can't speak for the entire military at this time, gentlemen." The general was experienced at dealing with the press, but unfortunately his companions were not, and they persisted in speaking out of turn. And now all three were waiting for the light to change, trapped at the crosswalk, easy prey for the reporters. "I must disagree with these gentlemen presently, until we... until this is irrefutably proved."

"Everything is being done that can be done." Again the clean-shaven man tried to put the conversation to bed, but his uncertain tone undermined his efforts.

The traffic light changed. "We'll have to hurry for our next meeting." The refuge of the car was in sight. The general picked up his pace.

Quinn realized he wasn't going to get anything of substance from the general, so shifted his focus to the bearded man. "Professor, you feel that there is a definite connection between..."

"A definite connection as far as Dr. Keller and myself..."

"Doctor, please." The general once again interrupted. "I thought we decided that is not proved yet."

The audience now knew the men flanking the general were both doctors of some kind. Scientists? Medical doctors? Whoever they were, they moved quickly, almost jogging toward the car.

As he trotted along, Quinn searched for a question to elicit just what the government knew about the strange, murderous outbreak. "Was it... Was the satellite... When the satellite was exploded..."

"It was an unusual amount of radiation," the bearded doctor replied. "Enough to cause mutation under certain circumstances."

"Could have happened to have a bearing on it," the general conceded.

"It does seem to have a bearing on it," the clean-shaven doctor chimed in.

The military sedan was now just yards away. A ramrod-straight soldier standing at the rear passenger door saluted as the general approached. The general saluted in return, and the soldier reached over and opened the door for the trio. First the bearded doctor, then the general, then the clean-shaven doctor climbed into the car, jostling each other as they settled in.

Quinn and the other reporters surrounded the car like hungry hyenas. "Will there be a reply for the press?"

"Later," the general confirmed, even though he had no idea when they'd release a report to the press.

"There will be a reply?" Quinn asked again.

"Yes."

Quinn pressed harder. He wanted something firmly on the record. "Later this afternoon? There will be a report this afternoon?"

As the soldier forced the door closed, the clean-shaven doctor, vexed by the onslaught of questions and the general aggressiveness of the reporters, found himself pinned inside the car against the open window. As all three microphones were thrust toward his face, he once again tried to mollify the beasts.

"Perhaps there will be a report later..."

"Later," the general interjected again.

"Will you close the window?" the clean-shaven doctor pleaded with the soldier, who had taken his position at the steering wheel. He turned to Don Quinn to make one last statement as the window ascended.

"We are doing everything possible to solve the problem," he insisted.

WHAT NEXT?

As the newscast cut back to the studio from the filmed report, the five people staring at the television in the dining room considered the scant new information and conspicuous absence of answers… with the exception of the most horrifying answer of all. *The wave of murder, which is sweeping the eastern third of the nation, is being committed by creatures that feast upon the flesh of their victims…*

For Ben, what little was said was enough to convince him the best course of action was to leave. "We have to try to get out of here."

"He said the rescue stations have doctors and medical supplies." Helen was also convinced. She turned to her husband. "If we can get Karen there, we can get help for her."

"*…is one of the world's foremost authorities on space science and technology. We expect that interview at any moment…*"

The newscaster filled time before the next segment, but Ben's attention was fixed on the rescue stations listed at the bottom of the screen. *Willard, Willard Medical Center...*

"'Willard,'" Ben read. His memory was jogged. "I saw a sign that said 'Willard.'"

"It's only about seventeen miles from here," Tom replied.

"You know this area. Are you from around here?"

"Judy and I are both from around here. We were on our way up to the lake to go swimming," Tom explained. "Judy had a radio, and we heard the first reports about this. So we knew the old house was here and we came in, and found the lady upstairs, dead." He nodded toward Cooper and Helen. "Then these other people came. We went down into the basement and put a bar across the door, and it is pretty strong."

"...guest we've been expecting has arrived..."

"How could we possibly get away from here?" Cooper interjected. Helen studied the television, ignoring her husband's pessimism. "We've got a sick child, two women, one woman out of her head, three men, and the place is surrounded with these things."

"...physiological research experiments conducted in the field for NASA."

The picture on the television widened to reveal the subject of the news anchor's introduction: a man in a dark suit with an academic air. The anchor turned from the camera and addressed his guest.

"Dr. Grimes, your entire staff, I know, has been working very hard to find some solution to these things that are happening. Do you have any answers at this time?"

"Yes, we have some answers. But first let me stress the importance of seeking medical attention for anyone who's been

injured in any way. We don't know yet what complications might result from such injuries."

Helen's expression flattened as her mind erupted with the implications of Dr. Grimes' statement: Her daughter's injuries weren't only caused by one of those horrible things, they could lead to her becoming one of them as well. The thought of her child attacking, killing, *eating* the flesh of someone repulsed and terrified her.

Ben caught Helen's stunned expression. "How bad has your kid been hurt?" he asked bluntly. Helen was caught off guard. She struggled to respond. *How bad is she hurt? What is he getting at?* She shrugged weakly.

"Look," Ben cut in before she could answer. "You go down there and tell..." he turned to Tom. "Judy?" Tom nodded. "Yeah, you tell Judy to come up here and you stay with the kid, all right?" Helen nodded, relieved to be given an excuse to return to her daughter. She hopped up from her chair and headed down into the cellar.

"In the cold room at the university, we had a cadaver. A cadaver from which all four limbs had been amputated. Sometime early this morning, it opened its eyes and began to move its trunk. It was dead, but it opened its eyes and tried to move..."

I HURT

Helen hustled down the steps. The information from the news took root in her mind, and she was unable to stop herself from indulging in the most horrific of possible scenarios involving her daughter. The news anchor's reports, the doctor's experiments, the three men in Washington D.C. and their outer-space theories... All the possibilities grew like weeds in her gray matter, choking out hope as images of her little girl — dead but still alive, tearing apart human flesh — filled every available space. What if the worst happened? What if they were forced to... to do something? *He said they chopped off its arms and legs... It kept moving... How could we ever...?*

Judy was sitting next to the makeshift table, dutifully watching the Coopers' motionless daughter. Helen touched her shoulder with an unspoken "thank you" as she approached. "They want you upstairs." Judy nodded and stepped out of the way as Helen gently placed her hands on the coat covering her child. "Did she ask for me?"

Judy shook her head. "She hasn't said anything."

Helen frowned. "I don't understand." Despite the awful thoughts pushing their way to the front of her mind, at her core she'd been certain she would return to find Karen awake, alert, and on the road to recovery. Instead...

Helen gently shook the comatose girl. Her whole body was still warm to the touch. "Baby?"

Karen didn't want to open her eyes. She was tired. *Too tired, mommy...* And thirsty. She wanted to sleep. But her mother shook her again, and that made her ache all over.

"It's mommy..."

Karen opened her eyes, which was hard because she was tired and her eyes felt like they wanted to stay closed. She was so sore. She couldn't see very well because the light was shining in her eyes. Everything was blurry. But she knew her mother was leaning over her. And someone else. Blurry. Someone behind her mother. She couldn't see who it was, but she didn't really care, because she was sick all over. She wanted her mother, but talking was hard because her mouth was so dry and she was so tired.

"I hurt..."

Helen's heart was broken. She couldn't stand to see her baby in pain. Her daughter was getting worse and... *Dammit, Harry, we need to get to one of those rescue stations...*

Judy placed a hand on Helen's back. The gesture felt awkward, as she didn't really know this woman or her daughter. But at that moment she felt a comforting gesture was important. *Poor Helen... Poor little girl...* "I'll come back down as soon as I find out what they want."

Helen nodded. "Thank you, Judy." She smoothed Karen's hair as Judy climbed the stairs and left mother and daughter alone in the cellar.

SOAK THEM WITH GASOLINE AND BURN THEM

Back in the newsroom, Dr. Grimes continued his tutorial on the disposal of recently deceased loved ones. A purely pragmatic man, he didn't fully appreciate the effect his recommendations were having on a more emotional audience.

"The bodies should be disposed of at once," he stated matter-of-factly. "Preferably by cremation."

The news anchor felt he had a responsibility to inform his viewers in a truthful manner, but there was a method for delivering uncomfortable information to a family audience, and he had a gut feeling this conversation was about to take a turn in the opposite direction. Disposed of at once? Cremated? "Well, how long after death, then, does the body become reactivated?"

"It's only a matter of minutes."

"Minutes?" The news anchor was shocked. Surely Dr. Grimes wasn't suggesting families should dispose of their own corpses. "That doesn't give people time to make any arrangements…"

"No, you're right," interrupted Dr. Grimes. "It doesn't give them time to make funeral arrangements. The bodies must be carried to the street and burned. They must be burned immediately."

Dr. Grimes became agitated. He wasn't upset at the thought of burning bodies. He was upset at the reaction from the gentleman seated across from him. *Why can't he understand? It's simple math…*

"Soak them with gasoline and burn them," he insisted. "The bereaved will have to forgo the dubious comforts that a funeral service will give. They're just dead flesh. And dangerous."

THE PLAN

Ben forged ahead with his plan. Cooper wasn't going to lead, Tom was too young and indecisive — and honestly, Ben liked being in charge. Having a course of action felt like the best defense against the monsters outside, and of all the people in the house he was the only one who was thinking logically. Cooper and his wife had the kid. Tom had Judy. The woman on the couch could talk only about her brother, when she talked at all. Ben was the only one who didn't have to consider someone else, so he could look at the situation with an unbiased eye and see what was best. And what was best right now was getting out of the house.

The first task was to fill the truck with gasoline. Ben figured out a plan that would allow even that coward Cooper to help. He caught Judy just as she emerged from the cellar. "Judy, I need you to find some bedspreads or sheets to tear up into small strips, okay?" She nodded.

Ben turned to Tom. "Is there a fruit cellar here?"

Tom nodded. "Yes."

"We need some bottles or jars to make Molotov cocktails to hold them off while we try to escape."

"Hey!" Tom suddenly remembered an important item in the cellar's inventory. "There's a big can of kerosene down there."

Judy headed for the main hallway stairs. "I'll see what I can find."

"I'll look for the bottles." Tom turned toward the cellar door when Cooper stopped him.

"There's a big key ring down there," Cooper offered grudgingly. "There may be a key to the gas pump on it." Cooper and Ben exchanged a look.

"I'll check." Tom disappeared into the cellar.

Ben and Cooper were left alone in the dining room, save for the silent presence of the woman on the couch. Ben kept his body language nonconfrontational. Cooper kept his mouth shut. They both understood Ben was the king of this part of the castle. An uneasy truce, if only for the moment.

"We can toss the cocktails from a window upstairs." By "we" Ben meant Cooper. He knew he'd never be able to talk the man into helping with the truck outside. "Meantime, a couple of us can go out and try to get the gas, then we can come back for the rest of the people."

Ever vigilant, Cooper found the flaw in Ben's plan and pounced. "But that'll leave a door open someplace!"

"Yeah, that's right," Ben replied evenly. Even Cooper could be right once in awhile. "It better be this door," he said, pointing to the door that led to the porch. "It's closer to the truck. Before we go out, we'll put some supplies behind the cellar door. While we're gone, the rest of you can hole up in there."

Tom returned from the basement carrying a box. "I found some fruit jars in the cellar." He set the box down and pulled a key ring out of his pocket. "And there's a key on here that's labeled for the gas pump out back."

Ben's demeanor took an unusually uncertain turn as he thought through the next steps. "I'm not really that used to the truck. I found it abandoned."

Tom brushed off Ben's concern. "I can handle the truck, no sweat."

Ben fished the truck keys out of his pocket and handed them to Tom. "You're it, then. You and I'll go." Ben and Tom shared a solemn look. Coming up with the plan hadn't been any harder for Ben than submitting their situation to logical thought, and Tom had volunteered to drive without hesitation. But leaving the safety of the house had been an idea, a plan, a concept until now. Handing the keys to Tom meant they were actually going outside. And that scared both of them.

Cooper watched the unspoken exchange with a mixture of anger and jealousy. *As if they're the only brave men in the house... If they get themselves killed, I was right, and we'll stay in the basement for as long as it takes...*

Ben laid out the rest of his plan. "We'll put whatever lumber we find behind the cellar door." He turned to Cooper. "You can go upstairs and toss the cocktails from a window." He waited for Cooper's refusal or critical assessment of his instructions, but the man just nodded stoically. "Tom, you and I will have to unboard this door." Again he turned to Cooper, this time allowing his tone to carry the hint of a threat. "After you toss the cocktails, you hustle back down here and lock this door." *Don't mess this up, Cooper...* "It's no good to board it up because we'll have to get back in quickly." *And don't even think about locking us out...*

Once again Cooper reluctantly nodded. Part of him knew the plan could save their lives. But part of him still believed the cellar was the safest option. And who did this guy think he was ordering all of them around? *You got it until it goes bad, then you're on your own...*

"After we get the gas and get back into the house, then we'll worry about getting everybody into the truck. Now, let's move it." Ben and Tom left the dining room to hunt for supplies. Cooper remained behind, grimly watching the television.

"There is no place to flee for safety, except for the rescue stations which have been set up. Indications are that before this emergency is over, we will need many, many more such rescue stations..."

WHY DO YOU
HAVE TO GO?

Judy sat in the den, scissors in hand, a small pile of fabric strips on her lap, a larger pile of sheets on the floor next to her. Alone for the first time in hours, she stared into space, grateful not to be in a room where she was treated like a silly girl, or her opinion automatically discounted by never being requested. The Coopers constant bickering drove her crazy, and Mr. Cooper was such a bully. That man Ben was okay, but bossy. Even Tom was starting to act like Mr. Cooper, telling her what to do like he was her father. And that woman on the couch…

Can't we just stay in the basement?

Tom walked into the den carrying a jar of kerosene for the Molotov cocktails. Judy smiled at him. He half smiled back. "You always have a smile for me," he said kindly. As he sat down at the table the smile slipped from his face. Maybe the situation in which they found themselves had worn down his own typically upbeat attitude, but for some reason, at this moment, his girlfriend's positive behavior seemed out of place. "How can you smile like that all the time?" he asked. An accusatory tone crept into his voice, which he tried to play off as a joke. Judy didn't respond. They both silently agreed to keep the peace.

"How many do you have done?" Judy handed him the few strips she'd cut from the sheets. "Come on, honey," Tom scolded. "We gotta move." He started dipping the strips into the kerosene.

Judy said nothing, just looked down at her hands. She didn't want to cut strips and she didn't want to make explosives. She wanted to take some food and put it in the cellar, watch the television for updates, and run down into the basement if the situation got bad upstairs.

They worked in silence for another minute, until the quiet felt too awkward. "Tom, are you sure about the phone?" she asked. She was more than capable of checking the phone herself, but this was the first topic she could think of that hadn't been gone over thoroughly by the men.

"The phone is dead out," he replied pointedly. Why wouldn't he be sure? "All you get is a recorded message."

"If I could only call the folks," she said sadly. "They're going to be so worried about us."

"Everything'll be all right," he said, once again sounding like her father.

How can he be so sure?

"As soon as we get to Willard, we'll call them." *Can't you figure this out by yourself?* He wanted to reassure her, but he felt like she wasn't listening. "They might even be there."

"I know," she replied glumly. They worked in silence for another few moments. "Tom..." She hesitated. She didn't want a lecture, but she was so unsure. The truck, the bombs they were making. The plan seemed so big when all they needed to do was wait. "Are you sure we're doing the right thing, Tom?"

"What, about getting outta here?"

"Yeah."

"Well, the television said that's the right thing to do. We've got to get to a rescue station."

"I don't know..."

"Come on, you're starting to sound like Mr. Cooper now."

That was mean... "But why do *you* have to go out there?" She was having a hard time expressing herself. Of course she wanted to leave, but not *this* way. Not *now*.

"Look, I know how to handle that truck. And I can handle the pump. Ben doesn't know anything about that stuff."

Judy didn't care what Ben knew or didn't know. She didn't know the man, and she was getting tired of having to just go along with whatever he said. *Don't I get a vote?* "But we're safe in here."

"For how long, honey?" *Can't she do the math?* "We're safe now. But there's gonna be more and more of those things."

"I know," she replied testily. "I know all that."

Tom shook his head and sighed a big *why won't you listen?* sigh. "Listen, remember when we had the big flood? Remember how difficult it was for us to convince you that it was right to leave? Remember?"

Judy looked away. She wasn't in the mood for his patronizing tone, and she knew what he was about to say.

Tom pressed on. "Remember we had to go to Willard then? This isn't a passing thing, honey. It... It's not like just a wind passing through. We've got to do something, and fast."

He was trying. She understood that. Despite treating her like a child at times, he did love her. And she loved him. She truly did. Even though she disagreed with the plan, the fact that he was doing it all for her made her love him even more. She had to hug him, and she did. Tightly.

"I just don't want you to go out there, that's all," she said, her face pressed against his neck. The tears started to flow.

Tom could feel her crying against him. "Hey... Smile, honey. Where's that big smile for me?" He knew he'd been impatient with her — and even though he had the best of intentions, seeing her cry made him feel awful. "You sure are no use at all, are you?" he joked gently. "We've got work to do, honey."

She pulled back and looked him in the eyes. He could see that she wasn't just sad. She was terrified.

He tried to continue his train of thought. "And you...
You..."

But it became impossible not to kiss her. And so he did.

ON YOUR MARK

Ben, Tom, Judy, and Barbara by default, gathered in the dining room and waited for Cooper to return.

As Cooper stepped up from the cellar, where he'd been stockpiling food, Ben handed him a box full of Molotov cocktails, which he accepted without argument. At least verbally. *You better hope this works, Buster, or you're outside with those things and I'm in the cellar.* He was about to make his way to the upstairs bedroom when he realized the silent woman on the couch was probably unaware of the situation about to unfold.

"We better get her downstairs." *Of course she's not listening. Jesus Christ…*

Judy leaned in. "We have to go downstairs now, Barbara." Barbara looked back at Judy blankly, then she shifted her gaze to Ben. An unspoken question knit her brow.

Ben knelt in front of the dumbfounded woman. "She's right. You have to go downstairs now. Just for a little while, until we get back." Barbara's reply was continued silence, mixed with a complete lack of comprehension. Ben didn't want to physically drag her down the stairs, so he tried again. "Then we can all leave," he offered as further explanation.

Leave? "Oh, I'd like to leave. Yes…" Barbara wasn't sure how going down into the basement would help them leave, but that man seemed so sure, and she desperately wanted to believe him. She stood up and Ben guided her toward the cellar door. Judy retrieved Barbara's coat from the couch and followed her down the stairs. Cooper, jittery, still with little confidence in the plan, exited the dining room and climbed the stairway to the second floor.

Ben met Tom at the door to the porch. His pace across the short distance from where he stood to where Tom waited was slow, deliberate, hesitant. Despite having rallied the household around this plan, he was in no hurry to open the door. The number of creatures had tripled over the last few hours. Even if he and Tom managed to gas up the truck and get back to the house without being dragged off to their deaths, there was no guarantee those things wouldn't congregate and flip the vehicle over once they locked themselves back inside.

The younger man held out a hammer. Ben nodded stoically and took the tool from Tom's hand. Once again the two men contemplated the prospect of opening the door.

"Good luck," Ben offered with a forced casualness.

"Yeah." Tom's reply fell somewhere between *Thanks* and *Don't count on it*. Luck had been in short supply over the last twelve hours.

The two men set to work, Ben using the hammer and Tom using a crowbar to pry off the boards Ben had placed so strategically just hours earlier. They tried to work as quietly as possible, but noise was inevitable when yanking nails out of a wall.

As they pushed the last boards aside, Tom noticed movement out of the corner of his eye. He turned to find Judy standing in the cellar doorway. Her face told him how scared she was, how much she loved him, and how unhappy she was they were going to be separated during the mission. But she offered him the tiniest smile, just like he'd asked her to earlier. He smiled back. *It's going to be okay, honey...*

Upstairs, Cooper installed himself at a window overlooking the front yard. He folded the curtains out of the way, then pushed the pane up and removed the screen. The fact the upstairs windows weren't boarded up wasn't lost on him. *Perfectly safe, huh? What if those things can climb?* But he'd agreed to do his part to help, so he prepped the Molotov cocktails and waited for the signal from down below. *He doesn't understand. I'm not a bad guy. I just want us to be safe...*

Outside, the horde of flesheaters was agitated. Their number had increased to more than three-dozen, and the sounds of the wooden barricade being dismantled had drawn their attention toward the house. They still wandered aimlessly, but their movements were sharper, more frantic. More anticipatory.

Downstairs Ben entered the dining room with another table-leg torch already ablaze. "You ready upstairs?" he called to Cooper.

"Yes!"

"Okay, toss 'em!"

Cooper struck a match and touched the flame to the wick of a Molotov cocktail. The kerosene-soaked fabric caught fire immediately, burning more rapidly than he had anticipated. Being careful not to allow the flames to spread to the walls or curtains, Cooper slung the blazing jar out the window.

The first cocktail hit the ground five feet in front of the truck and shattered, splashing flaming kerosene across the grass. The ghouls nearest the truck staggered backwards, moaning their discontent as they shielded their eyes. The second cocktail smashed to pieces at the right side of the truck, causing the gathered flesheaters to again shift their positions. The third cocktail exploded on the lawn closer to the house, driving back another small group.

The fourth and final cocktail landed in the middle of a group of the ghouls, right at the feet of Mr. Upshaw, the floor manager of a family-owned nursery a half-mile outside of Evans. He'd been carrying a bag of grass seed out to the Tomaselli's truck when Dan Adams (who'd suffered a heart attack earlier in the day) and Missy Thomas (who'd taken a full prescription of Valium with half a bottle of vodka the night before) met him in the parking lot at the end of his shift. After a day of wandering the countryside, he'd found himself at Edgar's farmhouse, and now he was the target of Cooper's final Molotov cocktail.

Mr. Upshaw staggered away from the farmhouse, covered in flames. The gathered crowd of flesheaters lost interest in the house, and instead focused on getting away from the scattered — and roving — fires.

Cooper bolted down the stairs and into the dining room. "Go ahead! Go on!" he shouted at Ben and Tom.

From the cellar door, Judy watched Tom unbolt the front door and dash out toward the truck. *Wait!* Ben followed with the torch in one hand and the shotgun in the other.

Outside the house Tom raced to the truck, while Ben hung back a few feet, keeping himself between the flesheaters and the porch. Just as Tom opened the truck door, Joe Meyer (who had been at the diner earlier) ran up and grabbed him. Tom shoved him away, unintentionally ripping the ghoul's shirt off as he did. Joe fell backwards onto the ground, giving Nick Brown (who'd had a brain aneurysm alone in his house yesterday morning) the opportunity to latch onto Tom as he tried to get into the cab. Tom put a foot on the ghoul's chest and shoved as hard as he could, propelling the flesheater back far enough for him to get the truck's door closed and locked.

Seconds later, the driver's side of the truck was crawling with dead adversaries. Ben quickly sidled up and crouched down on the passenger side, for the moment unseen by the horde.

Inside the dining room, Cooper watched the action, ready to slam the door shut the minute one of those things even halfway turned toward the house. *Dammit! They're all over the truck already!*

Judy gripped the frame of the cellar doorway, unconsciously digging her fingers into the cheap wood. She couldn't stand the thought of Tom being out there without her. She could hear the ghouls' moans, but not being able to see what they were doing drove her crazy.

Go!

She needed to get out of the house so she could see what was going on. So she could help. Yes, she could help!

Go!

He said to stay in the basement...

Go! Get out there!

It's dangerous...

Get. Out. There!

She made her decision and sprinted toward the front door. "I'm going with him!"

Cooper tried to grab her, to shove her away from the door so he could close it. *What the hell is she doing?!* "Get back in the cellar!" he shouted at her. She was frantic, wild. She slapped his hands away as he tried to keep her inside.

"I'm going!"

"It's too late. Too late!"

But she was already outside.

IT'S TOO LATE

"It's too late. Too late!"

Cooper grabbed at Judy as she ran out of the house, but stopped short of actually following her out the door. If the girl was determined to risk her life, he wasn't going to risk his to stop her.

Tom heard Cooper's shout over the moans of the flesheaters pounding on the driver's side window. His mouth dropped open in shock when he saw Judy dash out of the house. *What is she doing?*

As soon as she'd taken her first step off the porch, Judy knew that she'd made a mistake. She hadn't seen the creatures up close until now. Their faces were twisted and ugly, their mouths open like hungry animals. The way they swarmed the truck reminded her of rabid dogs, crazy and vicious. There was a bigger crowd in the yard than she'd imagined, and she didn't even have a weapon to defend herself. She turned to run back inside.

Slam!

Inside the house, Cooper slammed the door shut and turned the lock. *She wanted out? She's out.*

Judy froze in place, paralyzed with fear. *He locked me out!* She looked at Tom helplessly. *What do I do?!*

Tom's heart sank. There were too many of those things near the truck for him to get out and help. She was going to get killed, and he was going to have to sit and watch those things tear her apart.

"Well, if you're coming, come on!" Ben's voice broke the spell. He waved Judy over toward the truck. "Get in! Come on!" Judy ran toward Ben. He set the torch on the ground and shouldered the rifle while she climbed into the passenger side of the truck. As she pulled the door closed she looked at Tom, her expression begging his forgiveness for her rash decision to leave the house. *I'm sorry!* But Tom had no time to think about anything except getting the truck over to the gas pump.

Ben resisted actually firing the gun, worried the sound would draw so many of those things toward the truck that driving away would be impossible. But the time had come, and he drew down on Mrs. Whitehurst (she'd started laughing after taking a bite of her lunch yesterday, causing bread to get lodged in her windpipe) and shot a baseball-sized hole clean through her torso. This deterred her only for as long as she needed to regain her footing, and then she continued her pursuit of the people in the pickup.

Ben grabbed the torch and jumped into the bed of the truck as the flesheaters pushed in closer. Tom would have to back out instead of turning around, so Ben stood toward the rear of the pickup and waved the flames at the crowd.

Cooper peered out between the boards covering the dining-room window. His blood pressure rocketed as the creatures surrounded the truck. *There's too many of them! No way they're getting that truck out of there!* He was ready to barricade himself in the cellar, but something told him to wait. The flesheaters were all ignoring the house, but if that changed he'd head down to the basement like a shot.

Individually, the creatures shrank from the fire. But as their numbers increased, as the crowd became more dense, the mob was emboldened against the torch.

Ben touched the flame to the man from the cemetery, now just one attacker in a horde of killers. Tom and Judy would have recognized him as Ted Shiner, a teacher from the local high school. Two days ago he'd been to a funeral, and he'd lagged behind in the cemetery after everyone else left. Now his jacket went up in flames, and he backed away, batting at the fire on his chest, while the crowd pushed in and closed the gap left by his absence.

Tom threw the truck into reverse and hit the gas. As they backed away from the house, Ben leaned over the cab and waved the torch at the persistent flesheaters, but the flame was too far from the ghouls to pose any real threat. Several of them kept pace with the truck, banging on the hood and grabbing at the mirrors. Rob Johnson, who had also been at Beekman's Diner earlier, stumbled as he pursued the pickup. He grabbed the front bumper and was dragged along for a hundred feet until the bumpy terrain knocked him loose.

Tom backed the truck away as far as he could, then shifted into first gear and cranked the wheel to the left. Ben was thrown off balance in the bed as Tom made the turn, but he managed to keep himself upright with torch in his hand as they changed direction. Tom wanted to stomp on the gas pedal, but the smashed headlights prevented him from navigating as well as he'd like. The ground was so uneven he was afraid the truck would be irreparably damaged if he hit a gopher hole or a tree stump at full throttle, so he kept a steady speed as he rolled toward the gas pump and the barn.

The truck passed out of the area Cooper could monitor from the dining room, so he dashed into the kitchen for a better vantage point. Now he could see the pickup had pulled away from the main crowd of creatures, driving past the few stragglers on the way to the gas pump with ease. *They just might make it…*

Even at such a slow speed the pickup quickly outpaced the creatures. Within moments, Tom, Ben, and Judy arrived at the gas pump. Ben hopped out of the back and kept watch while Tom sprinted over to the pump with the key ring. Although they were in the clear at the moment, the crowd of three-dozen flesheaters was steadily making its way toward the truck. And who knew how many were gathered just beyond the house lights, hidden by the darkness? Ben figured it would be about two minutes before this became a very big problem. Stack enough of those things around the truck and they'd be trapped, unable to drive away even if they ran over a few. He set the torch down on the ground near the rear bumper as a deterrent, then turned to help Tom.

At the gas pump, Tom's shaking hands and racing mind kept him from accomplishing the simple task of inserting the key into the lock. *This isn't the key! It isn't the key!* He wasn't thinking clearly enough to realize he was trying to insert the key with the thread turned in the wrong direction. "This key won't work!" he shouted at Ben.

"Watch it." Ben pulled Tom away from the pump, then aimed the shotgun at the padlock without thinking. *Gotta stop wasting time!* His own panic had eroded his better judgment, and fired the gun not just at the lock, but the gas pump it protected. The blast blew the metal to pieces, miraculously without blowing them all to bits.

Tom grabbed for the nozzle. In his haste he accidentally wrapped his fingers not just around the handle but the lever as well. As he spun around, a stream of gasoline shot out, spilled on the ground, and drenched the rear passenger side of the pickup.

"Watch the torch!" Ben dove in to retrieve the flaming table leg from the ground, but he was too late. The gas on the ground caught fire and quickly spread to the truck. In seconds the rear panel and the tire were ablaze.

Cooper watched the truck catch fire from the kitchen window. His worst fears had been confirmed: This was a suicide mission. *It's over. Jesus Christ, they're dead already...*

For the first split second Tom didn't comprehend what had just happened. He tried to sidestep the flames so he could get close enough to insert the nozzle back into the gas tank. *I can't get this near the fire...* His thoughts finally caught up to events and he froze, now fully aware of the disaster unfolding in front of him. *The pump could blow! We have to move the truck!*

"We've gotta get away from the pump!" Tom called out to Ben. He re-cradled the nozzle and ran around to the driver's side of the truck.

Ben hadn't heard Tom call out to him, nor had he seen the younger man run back to the cab. He was too busy trying to smother the flames with an old moving blanket he'd grabbed from the bed of the pickup.

Judy was in a panic. She wanted to jump out, but the flames had grown and she was afraid she'd catch fire if she opened the door. She was just about to crawl out the driver's side when Tom jumped into the cab. "Hang on!" he shouted. He stomped on the clutch and turned the key. The engine growled to life. He jammed the stick shift into first gear, pressed the gas pedal, and released the clutch. The truck started to roll forward.

Ben was caught unaware when the truck shot forward. He stumbled backward, trying to stay away from the flames and avoid getting run over. *That fool!* "Stop!" he shouted. "Tom, you gotta get out of that truck!"

Cooper watched in horror as the pickup, still ablaze, rolled away from the barn. He couldn't tell if all of them were in the truck. Was Ben still over by the pump?

Tom sped away into the field just past the lawn. He knew the truck was probably going to burn up, but he had to get away from the pump or they'd have a huge explosion on their hands.

The fire near the barn was spreading. Ben beat at the flames with the blanket, desperately trying to keep them from igniting the pump or the fumes. Tom and Judy were on their own. There was no way he could help them now.

Tom looked back to the rear of the truck. The flames were spreading. The truck was going to be a total loss. But they were far enough away from the gas pump, and hopefully the field wasn't so dry that a grass fire would sweep the area. He slammed on the breaks. "Let's get outta here!" He threw open the driver's side door and jumped out. "Come on, come on!" He frantically gestured for Judy to slide across the seat and get out of the cab.

Judy leaned toward Tom, but she was pulled up short. Something held her back. Panic-stricken, she twisted around in her seat, frantically trying to figure out what was keeping her in the cab. *My jacket!* A loop on the waist of her jacket had twisted itself around the door handle when she'd gotten into the truck.

"My jacket's caught!" She tried to wriggle out of her jacket but the small cab left her no room to maneuver. Tom dove back into the truck to help her...

The flames penetrated the truck's fuel pump.

Womp!

The truck disappeared in a blanket of fire.

The explosion that engulfed the truck was loud, white hot, and instantaneous. Flames burst from the gas tank, through the engine block, up from under the steering column and dashboard filling the cab in a millisecond. Tom and Judy were burnt alive so quickly they had just enough time to take a single shocked breath that filled their lungs with fire. The scream that followed disintegrated in the flames. Their bodies roasted in the heat until their clothes were burned away, then their skin and muscles caught fire. The stomach-turning stench of scorched meat wafted into the air, mixing with the pungent aroma of hot metal, burning oil, and melted rubber.

Ben and Cooper shared a thought from their separate vantage points: *My God.*

LET ME IN

Ben stared at the fire, numb. The finality of the situation sank in.

Two people had been killed as he watched. *Tom and Judy are gone...*

They were killed during a plan he'd told them was their best option. *Cooper was right...*

Their only realistic means with which to travel to a rescue station had been destroyed. *The truck is gone...*

Ben hadn't known Tom and Judy very well. But they trusted him, and now they were dead. He felt lifeless inside, out of ideas and hope. As he stood, stunned, transfixed by the truck fire, Ben considered running. Just running away, into the fields, toward town, leaving the farmhouse and Cooper and the silent woman and the mother and the injured child behind. And if those things got him, well, then they got him.

A moan interrupted Ben's thoughts, all of which had run through his mind in the space of a few seconds. The crowd of flesheaters, not burdened by guilt or indecisiveness, had arrived at the barn. Ben was surrounded, and the realization there could be dozens, hundreds more of those things in the darkness of the field kept him from turning and running away. The house was the safest option, and he meant to take advantage of that fact.

Ben raised the gun and shot a hole through Hank Daley (a salesman who had discovered an unconscious woman at the edge of his used-car lot yesterday morning), the closest in the crowd. But Hank kept moving forward, as did the rest. Ben snatched up the torch and waved the flames at the creatures as he calculated his next move. The majority of the flesheaters he could see were bunched up around him, with some stragglers scattered across the yard. He would have to take advantage of their awkward gaits and relatively slow pace and sprint past them to the house.

He stepped toward the crowd and swung the torch back and forth. The ghouls were just ten, twenty feet away, rapidly closing in all around him. He had to keep moving, swinging the torch in all directions, to hold them at bay. He lunged toward the part of the crowd with the fewest creatures. As they backed away from the flames an opening was created, and Ben darted through. More ghouls closed in as the crowd he'd just escaped followed him toward the house. Ben shook the torch to the left, then to the right, clearing a path as the creatures momentarily cowered from the fire.

Ben criss-crossed the lawn. He assumed changing directions would slow the creatures' progress, and sure enough he finally outpaced the crowd and had a clear shot toward the house. The kitchen door was the closest entrance, but he and Tom hadn't unboarded that door before they left. He ran to the house and raced around to the front door, not knowing if he would run into one of those things on the other side of the blind corner.

To his relief, the front of the house was clear. "Let me in!" he yelled as he sprinted onto the porch. He hit the door full force, expecting Cooper to open it. But the door didn't budge. "Let me in!" he demanded.

Cooper watched the aftermath of the truck explosion long enough to see the flesheaters gather around Ben near the barn. That was all he needed to see. *He's dead, the idiot. Now we're trapped here without a vehicle if we need one!* He was headed back down to the cellar when he heard Ben banging on the door.

"Cooper!"

He stopped at the top of the cellar stairs and briefly considered unlocking the door. He quickly shook off that thought. There was no way in hell Cooper was going to open the door. Ben may have gotten to the porch, but there was no telling how many of those things were on his tail. Opening the door would be inviting them in, and he wasn't about to endanger his family to save some guy he didn't even know. *You screwed up. Live with it. Or don't.*

"Cooper!" Ben slammed his shoulder against the door again. Cooper instinctively ducked into the cellar stairway, fearing Ben would actually break down the door and catch him doing nothing. If he was downstairs he could say he thought Ben had been killed, and he hadn't heard him trying to get in. But against his better judgment, he stopped and watched the door.

On the porch, Ben was furious. Being obstinate was one thing, but leaving him out here to die was another. He mentally kicked himself for trusting Cooper with his safety. He rammed his shoulder against the door a third time, but no luck.

The flesheaters rounded the corner of the house and staggered up to the porch. Arms outstretched, they lurched straight toward Ben. He jabbed the torch at the closest one, using the table leg to shove the creature backwards off the stairs. The stumbling ghoul created a domino effect, causing those behind him to fall backwards as well. Ben threw the torch at the momentarily thwarted crowd, turned around, then reared back and kicked open the door with one solid blow.

He burst into the house to find Cooper ducking back into the cellar doorway. Cooper stopped, knowing he'd been caught acting like a coward. Ben shot the man a venomous look, but he couldn't take the time to deal with Cooper right now because the front door had to be rebarricaded against the horde of ghouls outside.

Ben slammed the door just as the creatures regained their footing and climbed up onto the porch. He hefted the spare closet door leaning against the wall, struggling to prop the cumbersome slab of wood across the dining-room entryway, using its full weight to keep the ghouls as bay. He held the door in place with his knee as he grabbed the hammer from the floor, then he searched his pockets for nails.

Cooper cowered in the cellar doorway, unsure of what to do. He knew Ben needed help, but what if those things overpowered them and broke into the house as they stood there? He also knew he was going to pay for leaving Ben outside, but there wasn't anything he could do about that now... unless he closed the cellar door...

He watched as Ben attempted to nail the door closed, but the ghouls' continued attack kept him from wielding the hammer properly. Guilt finally propelled Cooper from his safe zone. *Goddammit!* He rushed over and used his weight and strength to help steady the whole situation, which allowed Ben to nail the closet door across the entryway. The men worked together seamlessly, changing positions as needed to ensure the door was securely blocked.

Ben drove in the last nail. The pounding continued, but the door would keep the creatures out. For now.

Ben let the hammer drop to the floor. He turned to Cooper, jaw and fists clenched.

Cooper didn't move. He knew what was coming. *Just do it...*

Ben punched Cooper square in the face. Cooper rocked backwards, but Ben grabbed the front of his shirt and held him in place for a second punch. This time Cooper spun to the side and fell to the ground. He flipped over to his hands and knees and crawled like a child toward the den. As Cooper used the doorframe for leverage to pull himself to his feet, Ben stepped in and punched him again, landing a solid blow to the side of his face. Cooper fell back to the ground and quickly scampered away. Ben leaned in, latched onto the back of Cooper's shirt, and yanked him to his feet. Cooper tried to protect himself as

Ben swung a roundhouse toward his face, but fist met jaw, hard, once again, and Cooper was knocked to the floor. Now he was trapped, wedged between two overstuffed chairs in the corner, flailing his arms in an attempt to escape further punishment.

Ben reached down one last time, grabbed two handfuls of Cooper's shirt, hauled him up, and shoved him onto one of the chairs. Blood flowed freely from Cooper's nose.

Ben leaned in close, pinning Cooper's arms and screaming at him, inches from his face. "I ought to drag you out there and feed you to those things!" With one last shove, Ben released Cooper and stomped away. Cooper was left out of breath on the chair, his mind racing.

We can't stay here.

No, he *can't stay here.*

I have to get that guy away from us…

I have to get that gun…

INTERMISSION

The smell of cooked meat led them from the farmhouse, across the yard, and into the field where the pickup smoldered as the last flames burned themselves out. Now the creatures had easy access to what they craved: human flesh.

They crowded around the truck, pulled open the doors. Some climbed up onto the bed to reach through the now-broken rear window. Facing no fire, no gunshots, and no improvised barricades, the mob greedily tore apart what was left of Tom and Judy's bodies.

They ignored the red-hot metal that seared their own flesh as they tore muscles from bones, wrenched bones from sockets, twisted ligaments to the breaking point.

Sally Ann McCallister, who had been at her twenty-first birthday party just hours ago, reached in and clawed off a handful of meat from Tom's back, then toddled away as she bit off a mouthful and chewed voraciously.

As she made her way across the grass she passed Kathy Redmon, who was wearing a nightgown because she'd slept in with a cold and had been awakened by strange noises in her backyard. Kathy gnawed on a tibia, methodically cleaning the bone of every bit of muscle and tendon.

Closer to the house, Sonny Lennox and Norbert Donahue, two men who'd never met until tonight, fought over a wet pile of small intestines. Sonny successfully fended off the other man, then he eagerly shoved the innards into his mouth, not noticing or caring about the grass and dirt that covered the offal.

A city councilman gorged himself on a fresh liver.

A postal worker from two towns away scraped the flesh from a broken segment of a spinal column with her teeth.

A patient from the local hospital held up Judy's hand, the one part of either body not burned beyond recognition. He pulled the skin off with his teeth and held the hand out in front of his face, its fingers demurely pointed down. He appeared to be studying the dismembered body part as he chewed. At a distance, the scene looked like a grotesque parody of a marriage proposal.

Tom and Judy's bodies — organs, bones, skin, and muscles — would be spread out, strewn across the area in a larger radius than any explosion could have scattered them. Their bodies would be dismantled, consumed, digested in a brutal ceremony of hunger.

Tom and Judy would be deconstructed as human beings, reduced to parts, refuse, scraps. Their essence would evaporate.

And then the flesheaters would turn their attention back to the farmhouse.

OPTIONS

Ben wasn't sure how long he'd been looking through the dining-room window, watching the creatures as they ate Tom and Judy's remains. Twenty minutes? Half an hour? An hour?

Watching them feed was mesmerizing, like watching a car wreck in slow motion. At first he tried to look away, but then forced himself to watch as punishment for his hand in their deaths. Eventually he tired of the languid horror show and turned away. He sat on one of the dining chairs and reloaded the shotgun. The flesheaters would be done with their leisurely feast soon enough, which meant he had to be ready. There were now two fewer people to fight them off.

Cooper sat silently, nursing his bruised and bloodied face with a wadded-up kitchen towel. His eyes were cast down, but he was acutely aware of what Ben was doing with the shotgun. Cooper planned to grab that gun the minute it was out of Ben's hands. And then he and Helen were going down into the cellar, and Ben could rot up here with those creatures.

"Isn't it three o'clock yet?" Helen stepped into the dining room from the cellar stairway, rubbing her temples. Her head was throbbing, and seeing her husband sulking and Ben glowering only made her headache worse. As did being ignored by the two men. She tried again. "There's supposed to be another broadcast at three o'clock."

"Ten minutes," Cooper growled.

"Oh? Only ten more minutes?" Barbara, who had barely spoken since being sent down to the basement, was now back on the couch. The prospect of something happening brought her back into the conversation. "We don't have very long to wait," she said firmly. "We can leave." She paused for a moment, and when she spoke again, her voice had a slight tremble. "Or we better leave soon. It's ten minutes to three."

Ben finished loading the gun. He'd had enough idle chat; he was ready to take action again. Sitting around staring at each other wasn't going to get them to a rescue station. "You know anything about this area at all?" he asked Helen. "I mean, is Willard the nearest town?"

"I don't know," she shrugged. "We were just trying to get to a motel before dark."

Ben suddenly remembered the Coopers had driven to the farmhouse, or at least to somewhere nearby. "You said those things turned your car over. You think we can get it back on its wheels and drive it? Where is it?"

"Seems like it was pretty far away. Seems like we ran..."

"Forget it." Cooper cut her off tersely. *If you want answers, you're gonna talk to me.* "It's at least a mile."

"Johnny has the keys," Barbara offered.

"You're going to carry that child a mile?" Cooper shot back, mistakenly assuming Barbara was somehow advocating the plan. "Through that army of things out there?"

"I can carry the kid," Ben interjected. Cooper shot him a poisonous look. *Go to Hell.* Ben ignored him and once again directed his questions to Helen. "What's wrong with her? How'd she get hurt?"

"One of those things grabbed her..."

"Bit her on the arm," Cooper interrupted again. Ben rolled his eyes and shook his head in a way that let the Coopers know he thought they were idiots.

Helen was confused. "What's wrong?"

"Who knows what kind of disease those things carry?" Ben scolded her. Helen just stared at him. "Is she conscious?" he barked at her.

Helen was taken aback by Ben's aggressive tone. "Barely," she replied, a question in her voice. *What is he getting at?*

"She can't walk," Cooper insisted. "She's too weak."

Ben stewed. For once he couldn't blame his anger on Cooper, which made him even angrier. He refused to believe they had no options other than locking themselves in that damned cellar. "Well, one of us could try to get to the car," he practically shouted.

"You gonna turn it over by yourself?" asked Cooper smugly. Ben looked away. *That shut him up*, Cooper thought.

Ben was stumped until he realized what Barbara had just said. *Johnny has the key.* Johnny was her brother. Of course they had a car! He knelt down in front of her and asked as gently as he could, "You have a car? Where? Where is it?"

"You won't be able to start it," she replied in a singsong voice, as if speaking in a dream.

"Yeah, I know. But where is it?"

A chorus of moans emanated from outside, interrupting Ben's interrogation. He and Cooper jumped up from their respective seats and rushed over to the window.

The source of the moans was another squabble over Tom and Judy's remains, this time between a secretary from an insurance firm, a drifter who had jumped out of a boxcar at the railroad station three miles away, and the city clerk from Willard. Their aggravated noises caused an empathetic ripple among the flesheaters, who groaned and murmured as they continued their gruesome picnic.

Ben moved away from the window to turn on the television, but Cooper couldn't drag himself away from the horror taking place on the lawn. As he watched the flesheaters fighting over intestines and chewing on human bones like dogs, his stomach turned. He thought of Tom and Judy, two kids who had helped him secure the basement, good kids torn apart by those maniacs.

Now they were meat. Just meat. And it was Ben's fault. Cooper felt his gorge rise.

"Good lord…"

He closed his eyes, gritted his teeth, and fought the impulse to vomit.

THEY'RE ALL
MESSED UP

Cooper pulled himself away from the window. The revulsion he felt at the grisly scene outside didn't prevent him from doing some quick math. There were definitely more of those things out there than before the failed attempt at fueling the truck. Were they drawn by the sound? Or by the light? Cooper didn't know — but he was certain that, as long as he and the others were in the house, the number of those ghouls outside would only grow.

Ben tuned in the television. The same news anchor, tired but attentive, spoke to the camera.

"...being monitored closely by scientists at all the radiation detection stations. At this hour, they report the level of the mysterious radiation continues to increase steadily. So long as this situation remains, government spokesmen warn that dead bodies will continue to be transformed into the flesh-eating ghouls. All persons who die during this crisis, from whatever

cause, will come back to life to seek human victims unless their bodies are first disposed of by cremation."

Ben, Cooper, Helen, and even Barbara's spirits sank at this information. The situation just wasn't going to get any better. Cooper paced back and forth while the others sat quietly, grateful for the broadcast, but more depressed than ever at its content.

"Our news cameras have just returned from covering such a search-and-destroy operation against the ghouls, this one conducted by Sheriff Connor McClellan in Butler County, Pennsylvania. So now let's go to that film report."

The broadcast cut from the newsroom to a film of the Pennsylvania countryside. The first wide shot revealed an open field with a police cruiser in the foreground and men walking toward the camera in the far background. The quality of the light and position of the sun suggested the film had been shot late in the afternoon.

"All law enforcement agencies and the military have been organized to search out and destroy the marauding ghouls," the news anchor narrated over footage of several dozen civilians carrying rifles, shotguns, and handguns as they arrived at the home base in the countryside run by the military and sheriff's department in tandem. Some were dressed as if they lived in rural areas — flannel jackets, bluejeans, hunting caps — while others looked as if they'd just stepped out of their offices. Many of the men looked grim, deep in concentration, while others could barely contain their glee at being part of this newly formed militia.

"The survival command center at the Pentagon has disclosed that a ghoul can be killed by a shot in the head or a heavy blow to the skull." Now local uniformed police and highway patrol officers mingled with the men, most smiling as if they were at a turkey hunt over Thanksgiving weekend.

"Officials are quoted as explaining that since the brain of a ghoul has been activated by the radiation, the plan is: Kill the brain and you kill the ghoul." The camera panned across a lineup of local men, all carrying guns, all obviously positioned for the shot. Some looked nervous, uncomfortable. Was their discomfort brought on by the camera or by the task at hand?

Reporter Bill Cardille waded into the fray. He made his way over to Sheriff McClellan, who was deep in conference with his men. The sheriff was a short, compact man with deep-set eyes and a thin mustache. Unlike the men he supervised, Sheriff McClellan had chosen not to wear a uniform. Instead he wore a casual jacket and a straw hat. If not for the bullet belt slung over his shoulder and his dour demeanor, he could have been mistaken for a door-to-door salesman.

A uniformed deputy stepped up to the sheriff. "Want anything from the supply wagon?"

"No, we're all right," McClellan replied. His attention was drawn off camera to one of his men in the field. *Son of a bitch, I've told them a hundred times...* "Hey, Cass!" he called out. "Put that thing all the way in the fire! We don't want it getting up again."

"All right," Cass called back. "I gotcha."

Cardille used the distraction to pull the sheriff into an interview. He held out his microphone and asked, "Chief McClellan, how's everything going?"

"Oh, things aren't going too bad. Men are taking it pretty good." McClellan spied a group of men in a weak formation in the distance. "You want to get on the other side of the road over there," he called out. His patience was wearing thin. Wrangling these gung-ho gun nuts along with his own men was going to be the death of him.

"Chief, do you think we'll be able to defeat these things?"

"Well, we killed nineteen of them today, right in this area," McClellan replied, intimating an affirmative response to the reporter's question. "Those last three we caught trying to claw their way into an abandoned shed. They must have thought somebody was in there. There wasn't, though. We heard 'em making all kind of noise. We came over and beat 'em off, blasted 'em down."

One of the posse called over, "Chief, as soon as you're finished, can I see you here?"

"Yeah, okay." McClellan was less than enthusiastic about having to babysit these grown men, but if he left them to carry out the plan by themselves, the countryside would be overrun with those mutant freaks. He was all that stood between success and defeat at the hands of those deformed creatures. McClellan took his job, and himself, very seriously.

"Chief, if I were surrounded by six or eight of these things, would I stand a chance with them?"

"Well, there's no problem. If you had a gun, shoot 'em in the head. That's a sure way to kill 'em. If you don't, get yourself a club or a torch. Beat 'em or burn 'em. They go up pretty easy." McClellan was hoping that more people would take his advice so they could be done with this foul business once and for all.

"Well, Chief McClellan, how long do you think it'll take until you get the situation under control?"

"Well, that's pretty hard to say." Despite his lack of experience with television people, McClellan knew better than to give a hard deadline in a situation like this. "We don't know how many of 'em there are. We know when we find 'em, we can kill 'em."

"Are they slow-moving, Chief?"

"Yeah, they're dead," McClellan explained. "They're all messed up."

"Well, in time, would you say you'd be able to wrap this up in twenty-four hours?"

"Well, we don't really know." McClellan evaded the question again even though he was confident this was a quick, one- to two-day job. "We know we'll be into it most of the night, probably into the early morning. We're working our way toward Willard and we'll team up with the National Guard over there, and then we'll be able to give a more definite view."

"Thank you very much, Chief McClellan."

The footage cut to Cardille standing in front of the command center, looking directly into the camera. "This is Bill Cardille, WIIC-TV 11 news."

The broadcast cut back to the live feed in the studio. "Thank you, Bill, for that report. Official spokesmen declined to speculate just how long it may take to kill off all the flesheaters so long as the heavy rain…"

And then the television and all the lights in the house went out.

I HAVE TO GET THAT GUN

Ben, Cooper, Helen, and Barbara all looked around the room, confused. The house was once again dark, and absolutely silent.

"Is the fuse box in the cellar?" asked Ben.

"I don't know," replied Cooper. Before he'd even finished his sentence Ben strode over to the cellar door and disappeared down into the pitch-black stairway.

The darkness made Cooper feel even more defenseless, jittery. "It... It... isn't the fuse...," he stammered to the air. A single fuse wouldn't supply the electricity to an entire house. "The power lines are down." Of course Ben wasn't listening to him, but he didn't care. An opportunity had arisen. He spun around to face Helen, now sitting on the arm of the couch next to the still-oblivious Barbara. He tried to keep his voice and body language calm, but firm.

"Helen," he said, looking her dead in the eye. *Steady, convince her with your tone.* "I have to get that gun."

Helen's jaw clenched. She was incensed, unable to believe what she was hearing. With everything that was happening, her husband was going to get into a fight over a loaded gun? "Haven't you had enough?" she spat at him furiously.

Cooper pleaded with Helen. "Two people are dead already on account of that guy." He had to convince her he was right so when he made his move she wouldn't be surprised. "Take a look out that window. Look at..."

Cooper stopped the second he saw Ben step in from the cellar. As his nemesis crossed the room to look out the window, Cooper exchanged looks with Helen. His eyes said: *You know I'm right.* Her eyes said: *Don't. Just don't.*

Outside Dan Hills, a handyman, picked up a large rock and carried it toward the house.

Jim Peterson, the bag boy from the market in Willard, picked up the dining-table leg Ben had used as a torch. He dragged the leg past the still-smoldering overstuffed chair and up onto the front porch, then weakly swung the weapon and struck the door.

Inside the dining room, everyone jumped at the sound of the table leg striking the front door.

The flesheaters were back at the house.

First there was one creature pounding on the door, thirty seconds later dozens of creatures were gathering two and three deep at every possible entryway. They beat the house with their fists, some attacking the doors and windows, others blindly striking the solid outer walls, despite the fact they offered no hope of entry regardless of the fury with which they were battered. The barricades rattled, shook, loosened. The ghouls' hungry, agonized moans formed an unnerving chorus that joined the percussive sounds of the physical attack. The house, silent and dark moments ago, was filled with a wretched cacophony of undiluted desire. The orchestra petrified the occupants within, for they knew that their flesh was the singular object of the creatures' cravings.

Dan Hills tossed his rock, awkwardly and with little force, at a dining room window. The glass pane shattered.

Ben quickly stepped over to the window and laid the shotgun across the boards, using the weapon as a crossbeam to help shore up the barricade. He leaned with all his weight, but without the glass each individual board was vulnerable to the ghouls' grasping hands.

Helen sprinted over and put her back against the front door, doing her best with her slight weight. The creatures pounded harder and harder, loosening the nails keeping the barricade in place with each blow. The top corner of the door, free of obstruction, wrenched inward each time the ghouls struck. Helen spun around and pushed back against their assault with her bare hands.

Ben used both of his hands, his gun, his knee, and his hip to keep the boards up and the flesheaters' hands out. But there were just too many of them, and too many spaces between the planks. They grabbed at him, just inches from making purchase with a handful of his clothing.

"Get over here, man!" Ben yelled at Cooper.

Cooper stood back and watched, silently willing the shotgun to fall from Ben's hands. *Drop the gun... Drop the gun...*

When Helen turned, she was horrified to see her husband standing motionless at the cellar door as she and Ben struggled to keep the ghouls from breaking into the house. *The coward! The coward!*

"Come on!" Ben pleaded again. Just then a flesheater's hand clamped down on one of the boards and yanked. The force of the pull ripped the nails holding the plank in place out of the wall. The resulting gap left more room for the ghouls to maneuver, putting the rest of the barricade in danger of being torn from the window. Terrified he was losing the battle, Ben dropped the gun so he could use both hands to keep the boards in place.

Cooper's eyes lit up. This was his chance. He locked eyes with his wife, still struggling with the door. She looked at the gun on the floor then quickly glanced back up at him. Her eyes begged her husband *Don't! For God's sake, don't!* But he didn't care. He knew she would keep her mouth shut until he had the gun. Cooper took a tentative step forward to see if Ben would notice, but the man was too busy fighting off the ghouls to pay attention. *Now! Do it now!*

Cooper lunged forward, snatched the weapon off the floor, and cocked it. Ben turned at the sound to find his adversary pointing the barrel of the gun at him. *Dammit!* He had no choice: He had to continue holding the wood planks across the window as Cooper slunk back toward the stairway.

"Go ahead!" Cooper shouted as he backed toward the basement door. "Go ahead! You wanna stay up here now? Helen, get in the cellar."

Helen refused to move. Her husband's actions scared her to death. She wouldn't be part of leaving someone up here to die. She just stared at him, mute with rage and shame.

Cooper was furious. "Get in the cellar now!" he ordered. "Move!" He gestured with the gun toward the door for emphasis.

Ben threw a plank at Cooper, hitting him in the arms. Cooper flinched, causing the gun to point back toward the wall and giving Ben the half-second he needed to launch himself at the man he was convinced was going to get them killed.

Helen watched in horror as Ben grabbed the shotgun with both hands, then played tug-of-war with Cooper until he was able to wrench the gun away and shove her husband to the floor.

Cooper crawled away from Ben toward the cellar door, his eyes never leaving the man or the gun he held. Against a backdrop of ghouls' hands tearing apart the window barricade, and his wife trying to keep the flesheaters from breaking down the door, Cooper watched Ben methodically cock the gun.

Helen gasped. *He's going to execute him!*

Ben coldly raised the shotgun...

No!

...and pulled the trigger.

The force of the bullet drove Cooper backward.

Helen screamed.

Searing pain started from a pinpoint in Cooper's gut and radiated out into every fiber of his body. He tried to stand, but his legs betrayed him, refusing to support his weight. He clung to the cellar doorway for support as he dragged himself to his feet. *You bastard... You'll die here, too...*

Ben stood motionless for a moment as smoke rose from the barrel of the gun. He had a split-second of doubt, but the noise from the ghouls drowned out any guilt he felt over shooting the man. Satisfied he'd taken care of Cooper for good, he turned away and returned to his battle with the angry flesheaters at the window.

Barbara watched all of this as she'd watched everything since arriving at the farmhouse: silently. But the horror of the situation, the maniacs pounding on the house, the man shooting the other man, the noise, oh, the noise and the darkness were all wearing at her. She clutched her head, hands covering her ears, eyes squeezed shut, trying to wish away the day and bring back her brother. *Why, Johnny? Why?*

Helen screamed again. The ghouls had broken down part of the door behind her. She wanted to rush to her husband's side to try to save his life, but there was no way she could do that without letting all of those things into the house. So she planted her feet and pushed her back against the barricade with all of her strength.

As she strained against the onslaught, unable to move lest death be welcomed into the farmhouse, Helen was forced to watch helplessly as her husband fell backwards into the cellar door and disappeared down the stairs.

THE DEATH OF HARRY COOPER

Cooper clutched his abdomen with one hand and steadied himself on the wall with the other. He half stepped, half slid down the cellar stairs. The hot pain he'd felt when the bullet penetrated his gut was fading, but the rest of his body was shutting down. His vision blurred, the strength in his arms and legs ebbed. He felt like he was drowning each time he took a breath.

Bastard...
Shot me...
Son of a bitch...
Gotta get into the cellar...
Safest place...
Helen...?
Karen...?

Cooper fell against the shelves at the bottom of the staircase. He wrapped his arms around the timber and held himself upright. His legs, still supporting his weight through sheer force of will, had gone numb.

Helen, get down here…

As his body slowed, his mind raced. He had to make a plan, get Helen down here, get back up the stairs and block that door, figure out a way to let rescuers know they were down here. Bring down some food, bring down the television, get Tom and Judy…

No, they're dead… That guy killed them…

Get to the rescue station, get medical attention for his daughter…

His heartbeat slowed, then stopped. Despite his failing vision in the dimly lit cellar, he could see the child, his child, the eleven-year-old girl he should have been protecting on the makeshift table in the middle of the room.

Karen…

Daddy's coming, sweetheart…

He let go of the shelves, leaned in, and let forward momentum carry him from the base of the stairs toward his daughter.

Daddy's here, sweetheart…

His knees buckled. He grabbed the center beam, which now supported both the ceiling and a dying man. He reached forward. Not close enough. Get closer. All of his goals and plans evaporated except one: He had to save his daughter.

He fell forward toward the little girl one last time.

Daddy's here…

Cooper collapsed to the ground, his outstretched hand slapping against the edge of the door upon which his daughter lay. Her body shifted, but the movement was due neither to regained consciousness nor her father's touch, but the jostling of the precarious table.

Karen Cooper had already died in the cellar of a remote farmhouse in Pennsylvania.

Harry Cooper would soon die on the floor of that same cellar.

THE ATTACK BEGINS

The flesheaters ripped away the front door piece by piece, tearing the thick wood to kindling with their bare hands.

Helen screamed as the ghouls reached in, clawed at her, grabbed her hair. The creatures were held at bay by the closet door nailed across the entryway, but they would force their way in soon enough, either via the doorway or through the window where Ben fought them off with diminishing success.

Helen batted at the eager, hungry hands, some pulling away with locks of her hair yanked out by the roots. She wanted to run to the cellar, to protect her daughter, but she knew if she moved away from the door the monsters would push inside so quickly they'd catch her in seconds. She had no choice but to stand her ground until she could figure out a way to escape.

As Helen and Ben fought against the tide of death, Barbara remained on the couch and let the chaos wash over her. The sounds, the shouting, the moans, the house rattling, the boards breaking, all liquefied into a storm of white noise that rained over her and methodically eroded her conscious thought. She retreated deeper and deeper into her mind, as if chased there by a wave flooding the farmhouse. Down to nothing, down to quiet. Down to the bottom of the well. *Oh, Johnny...*

The reality of the farmhouse mercifully softened, faded into the distance. She was untethered, absent from the angry, jagged edges and punishing conditions of this place of death. Down, further, quieter. Barbara was almost free. It would all be over soon...

And then a figure stepped into the open space at the front door, and Barbara froze.

The man from the cemetery, the man who attacked Johnny and followed her here. That man was crystal clear, reaching in through the shattered door, grasping at the air between them. His twisted, burnt face pierced through Barbara's protective haze and reattached her to the house. His presence pulled her up and out of her reverie. She wasn't going anywhere.

Barbara's consciousness returned to the dining room, to the ongoing assault, to the horror. She was now fully present for the first time since arriving at the farmhouse. And she was angry. Enraged. How dare these people attack them? These people had no right. *They have no right!* She was not going to sit by and let these monsters break into the house.

She was going to fight.

Her mind, finally freed from the paralyzing shock of the attack in the cemetery, absorbed the new information at lightning speed. There was a board at her feet, the same board Ben had thrown at Harry Cooper. Barbara picked up the plank and launched herself at the door. "No!" she screamed at the creatures. "No! No!" she shrieked at the man from the cemetery as she slammed the board against his hands and face.

Helen saw her chance. With Barbara defending the door, she could get to the basement without letting the monsters in. She dashed to the cellar door, leaving Barbara and Ben behind to fight the flesheaters.

I'm coming, Karen!

THE DEATH OF HELEN COOPER

Harry Cooper was dead. He lay on the floor of the cellar, next to the door-and-sawhorse cot, his face smooth and free of anger. He was finally at peace.

For the moment.

Karen Cooper had died earlier, while her father struggled over a gun and her mother fought to keep the growing crowd of flesheaters out of the house. She breathed her last breath moments before the shot rang out upstairs. Her heart had stopped. Her body had cooled.

But now Karen knelt over her father's body. Her hands and mouth were filled with bloody flesh torn from his arm. She chewed, swallowed, took another bite.

"Karen?"

Helen hurried down the stairway. She assumed her husband was dead, killed by the gunshot and the fall down the stairs. But what about her little girl? As Helen made the turn past the shelves at the bottom of the stairs, she was relieved to see her daughter was no longer lying on the door.

"Karen?" The girl was up. She was alive, thank God. But what was she doing? Helen saw her husband's body lying next to the table. *Is he alive?* She took a cautious step forward. "Karen...?"

Helen's daughter looked up. Blood dripped from her mouth. At the sight of her mother, Karen dropped a handful of her father's flesh and stood up. She reached out with her blood-covered hands, as if asking her mother for a hug. But her bared teeth, dripping gore and saliva, made it clear Karen wasn't looking for an embrace.

She wanted to feed.

"No..." Helen's heart sank as she backed away from her daughter. Her tears started to flow. After all that happened — the attacks, the fights, the murder of her husband — her little girl was dead. Helen shook her head. No, that wasn't right. Karen wasn't a little girl any more, and she wasn't dead. She was a thing. A monster. Something to be...

Cut their heads off... Burn them... Burn them on a pile like garbage...

"Oh, baby," Helen sobbed. "Baby..."

As much as she ached to hold her little girl, Helen backed away as Karen, like an unsteady wild animal cornering her prey, stalked her around the cellar. She had no choice but to back up, as the sounds of destruction from the dining room made it clear going upstairs was no longer an option. She maneuvered her way around the cot, then accidentally stepped on her husband's lifeless hand. Harry's bones crunched under her foot. She flinched and lost her balance. Her feet got tangled in Harry's outstretched arm, and before she could right herself she fell backwards onto the floor, wedged into a space next to one of the shelves.

Karen paused as she passed a collection of gardening tools hanging from homemade racks on the wall. Without any change of expression, as if by pure instinct, she reached up and chose a weapon: the trowel.

The young girl raised the tool high above her head as she approached her mother. Helen squirmed on the floor, unable to

believe what her daughter was about to do. She shook her head.
No... baby, no...

Karen slammed the trowel down into her mother's chest.
The dull point of the tool wedged between Helen's ribs,
cracking her sternum. Helen shrieked in pain. The girl pulled the
trowel out, and a stream of blood gushed from the wound.

No...

Karen drove the weapon down again, this time puncturing
her mother's lung. Blood gurgled up Helen's throat and out her
mouth as she moaned in pain.

...Karen...

Again the girl yanked the trowel out of Helen's chest. As
she swung the rusty instrument of death above her head for a
third blow, blood splattered on the wall like paint.

The trowel came down a fourth time, cutting into Helen's
abdomen, tearing through her internal organs. Her eyes rolled
back in their sockets as guttural sounds and blood flowed from
her mouth.

...baby...

...Harry...

Karen raised the trowel again. The last thing Helen saw
while she was alive was her daughter stabbing the trowel into
her chest.

...stop...

The fatal blow destroyed Helen's heart. But despite her
mother's loss of consciousness, Karen continued to
methodically eviscerate the dying body.

Helen's blood splattered the walls, running down the
cracked surface in rivulets, a grim imitation of a work of art.

JOHNNY'S RETURN

As he fought off the flesheater assault at the dining room window, Ben caught sight of Barbara. Unlike the frightened girl who dashed out of the house as he arrived, this woman was animated, screaming, fighting the creatures fearlessly at the front door. He admired her courage. *We just might get out of this alive...*

Barbara beat at the hands that reached through the doorway, shrieking at the ghouls defiantly. All of the information she'd been unable to process — news broadcasts, people in the house talking around her — rushed in and filled her mind.

That man killed Johnny...

That man was dead...

We must burn them...

They're eating their victims...

They mustn't get in...

They're trying to eat us...

Eat us...

So she fought. She could do nothing else. Johnny was gone, she'd never see him again. She had to fight, to escape, to survive. Get back home, back to their mother.

The closet-door barricade was starting to buckle, so she threw herself against the cracking wood. This put her closer to those greedy hands, but she had no choice. If the barricade did not hold, they were dead.

Where one was weak, many were strong. The crowd outside had finally grown too large for the number of nails holding the barricade in place across the doorway. With one final surge, the horde of ghouls shoved forward and pushed the closet door out of the way. Barbara was forced to retreat as the heavy slab of wood fell to the floor. The flesheaters finally had unobstructed access to the house.

"No!" she screamed at the ghouls defiantly. "No! No, get out!" she shouted as she stumbled back.

And then, at the front of the crowd, she saw him.

Johnny?

Barbara was rooted in place by the sight of her brother. The dried blood trailing from his broken nose to his shirt. His gray-yellow skin. A gash on his temple. In a moment that felt stretched beyond time, Barbara stared at him, willing him to look at her.

Johnny!

When he finally turned to face her, his dead eyes — his cold, dead eyes — locked with hers, and in doing so his gaze changed. This was neither a spark of recognition, nor relief at finding her. No, this was an instinctive reaction to a more brutal assessment of the woman before him. She was cattle, an object, something to destroy. And he was here to do just that.

Johnny reached out and grabbed Barbara by the front of her dress. "No, Johnny!" She beat at his hand and arm. "No!"

Ben turned to see the flesheater dragging her toward the door. He leapt over from the window and reached for her, but the ghoul pivoted, forcing Barbara backwards and out the door. Ben pummeled the creature's back, but a dozen or more of those things had her in their grip.

"Somebody help me!" Barbara cried, but there was no one to do so. Ben watched helplessly as Barbara valiantly fought against the tide, only to be swept out the door by the current of death.

Her screams filled the air as her head sank below the sea of hands, eager to tear her apart.

RETREAT

The window barricade Ben fought so hard to defend finally disintegrated. The flesheaters pushed in some of the boards, yanked others out, and as soon as the opening was big enough, they began to crawl into the house. The group that dragged Barbara to her death finally cleared away from the front door to divvy up their prize, allowing a second wave to pour in.

Ben had lost the battle. The time had come to lock himself in the cellar and wait out the war. He didn't know, or care, if Cooper survived being shot, but at least he could help Helen and their kid. And if Cooper was still alive down there — well, he could take care of that if he needed to.

As Ben backed toward the cellar doorway, he felt someone grab his wrist. He looked down and was horrified to discover a little girl digging her nails into his arm. Her skin sallow, her blood-covered mouth open. Her teeth bared, ready to bite. He wrenched himself free and grabbed her by the shoulders. As he held her at arm's length, she clawed at the air, maniacally trying to sink her nails into his face. Ben grimaced as he realized the animal with whom he was fighting was the Coopers' daughter.

Ben spun her around and tossed her onto the couch. He could easily have snapped her neck, but she was just a kid, and he couldn't bring himself to damage a young child like that, regardless of what the men on the news told him.

Ben backed into the cellar doorway and slammed the door just as the girl leapt off the couch and flung herself at him. She clawed at the closed door and was soon joined by a crowd of her fellow creatures as they flooded into the farmhouse.

On the other side of the door, Ben quickly slid the two-by-four beams into the cradles installed by Tom and Cooper. As the flesheaters pummeled the door with their fists and the occasional weapon, the boards shook violently. Ben had no idea how many of those things were in the house now, and he didn't know how many it would take to break down the dilapidated barricade. So he waited, gun drawn, ready to shoot his way out if it came to that.

The ghouls flooded the house, bumping into each other and the furniture as they aimlessly paced back and forth, their feeding instincts high but their opportunities low. The creatures that followed Ben to the cellar door soon lost interest, and they, too, began to stroll through the farmhouse in search of prey.

As the attacks on the cellar door subsided, Ben realized Cooper had been right: The cellar was the safest place.

THE RETURN OF HARRY AND HELEN COOPER

Ben backed slowly down the stairs, ready to run back up if the creatures became more energized and redoubled their efforts to break down the door. He spied Cooper lying on the floor. He shook his head. *You dumb bastard. We could have worked this out if you'd been a stand-up guy...*

Just as he realized his sanctuary was a little too quiet, he saw Helen, splayed out, lying against the wall like a sack of garbage, a bag of meat someone had thrown on the floor. Blood covered her torso, flowed from her mouth, seeped onto and between the dirty bricks of the floor. Sticking straight up out of her chest was a trowel, like a signpost or a gravestone signaling "Here is death." *My God, did her little girl do that to her?*

Cooper's eyes opened. Ben stepped back, startled, unnerved that the transformation was taking place right before his eyes. He readied the shotgun, unsure if Cooper would jump to his feet or rise slowly from death.

Cooper sat up, deliberately, with effort, as if he were pulling himself from a deep sleep. His face was blank, not yet frenzied like the things upstairs. He turned toward Ben, not calmly — which would suggest thought or intent — but perfunctorily. Cooper was now a thing, an object that moved and, given the chance, killed.

Ben cocked the shotgun and shot Cooper in the face. Cooper's body fell back to the floor. Ben cocked the gun, aimed, and pulled the trigger a second time. And a third. What was once Harry Cooper would rise no more.

Ben turned away from the body and leaned his forehead against the support beam. He understood what the experts had asked of him on television. And he'd shot a half dozen of those things in the last twelve hours. But this was the first he'd actually known. Cooper was a bastard, and he deserved what he'd gotten upstairs when he'd threatened Ben. But somehow dispatching this... this thing that looked like Cooper was different.

And then Ben realized the job wasn't finished. He turned his attention to Helen, still lying motionless on the floor. *Don't do it... Please don't do it...*

Helen's eyes popped open.

Ben cocked the shotgun and shot her in the head. Just once. He couldn't bear to pull the trigger again.

He threw the shotgun to the ground. Furious, terrified, saddened beyond belief, he tore the makeshift table apart, flinging the sawhorses across the room. He searched for more objects to destroy, but finally he just put his face into his hands and wept. The agony was too much to bear. How could he possibly live in a world where good people died and then had to be treated in such a gruesome and inhuman manner? What about his friends? His family? Would he have to do this to them someday? Was this his life now? Destroying people before they had a chance to destroy him?

The noise level from upstairs increased. More footsteps, faster, more moans. Because of the shots? Had they heard them? Ben searched for the gun, which he found in the corner. He cocked the weapon and positioned himself across the room from the cellar stairs.

If they were going to come after him, he wasn't going down without a fight.

Upstairs, the flesheaters continued to roam the farmhouse. With no prey in sight, some of them wandered back outside. Others walked in and out of rooms, bumping into each other and ricocheting in new directions.

And after a while, just like any other day, the sun came up.

MORNING

From the edge of the property, in the early morning light, the farmhouse looked just like an ordinary farmhouse. Empty. Quiet. There were no sounds, except for a light wind and the calls of various birds in the distance.

The interlopers were gone, as if their moans and shambling presence had burned off in the morning sun. If not for the scorched truck in the nearby field, and the remains of an overstuffed chair by the kitchen door, the site would have appeared to be an abandoned home, rather than a crime scene.

A helicopter cut across the sky, flying past the farmhouse and over the surrounding open field. As the pilot searched for a place to land, he could see a fire line of civilians and police, all carrying firearms, making their way across the countryside. Unlike the flesheating scavengers, these men were hunters.

The helicopter landed at a safe distance from Sheriff McClellan's home base, a bridge over a dry creek bed at the edge of the field. Unlike the day before, this command center was much better organized and well manned. There was a medical unit run by local doctors and nurses, which so far had treated several cases of poison ivy and dehydration, and one gunshot wound that could have been much worse. The sheriff's department brought out the K-9 unit, which was busily sniffing through the thick brush lining the edge of the field. And the general plan of attack had developed from yesterday's militia-minded free-for-all into the implementation of a map-based grid in coordination with the National Guard.

McClellan had spent the night directing the volunteers, organizing supplies, and working with the fire department to make sure the flesheaters' bodies were burned in a consistent and safe manner. Now, as he approached two men taking a break against a telephone pole, he was working on less than two hours' sleep.

"Hey, Vince, Mel, you wanna get about four or five men and a couple dogs? There's a house over here behind those trees. We wanna go check it out." *So get off your lazy asses...* The men nodded and headed over to the K-9 unit.

McClellan nodded a *Good morning* to Bill Cardille and a cameraman from WIIC-TV as they approached from the news van. "You still here, Bill?"

"Yeah, chief, we're going to stay with it till we meet up with the National Guard." Cardille took a drag on his first cigarette of the day.

McClellan gestured to the cup in the reporter's hand. "Where'd you get the coffee?"

"One of the volunteers." Cardille handed his styrofoam cup to McClellan. "You're doing all the work, you take it."

McClellan accepted the coffee gratefully. "Thank you." He gestured to the field. "We should be wrapped up here. About three or four more hours, we'll probably get into Willard's end. I guess you can go over there and meet the National Guard." He turned to a small group of volunteers leaning against a supply truck. "Nick, you and the rest of these men wanna come with me?" He walked away toward the field.

The cameraman leaned in to Cardille. "Bill, I'll check with the office to see what's happening."

"All right, Steve. Tell 'em we're going to stay with it, and everything appears to be under control."

The K-9 unit started barking and straining at their leashes. They seemed to have smelled something over near the farmhouse, at the edge of the field...

ONE FOR THE FIRE

Where am I?

Ben opened his eyes.

He was sitting on the stairs with his back against the cold cement wall, a shotgun across his knees.

The cellar…

He'd moved from his perch across the room to the bottom of the stairs before he'd fallen asleep a few hours ago. He reasoned being closer to the door was his best option in case someone made their way into the house… and survived.

The sound of barking dogs pulled his attention into focus. *A search party?*

In the field near the burnt truck, a fire line of armed lawmen and volunteers came upon Mrs. Anderson (a retired grandmother) and Jeffrey Sanders (who worked the shoe-rental desk at the bowling alley) shuffling toward the farmhouse. Two deputies drew their guns and quickly shot both of them in the head.

Definitely a search party... with guns. Should I...? Was that the police? Or just a bunch of random people with guns? After watching Cooper lose his mind, Ben wasn't sure he trusted anyone with a firearm.

A station wagon rolled up the road toward the farmhouse. McClellan, leading a group of men on foot, waved the car over.

"They need you down there by the barn." The driver signaled a thumbs-up and drove past the sheriff. McClellan turned to the group. "You guys can follow the wagon down. I only need a few men to check out the house." All but a handful of the men peeled off and followed the vehicle down the road. McClellan and his men continued walking toward the house. The sheriff jabbed a thumb toward the burnt-out truck as they passed. "Somebody had a cookout here, Vince."

"Yeah, sure looks like it," the sheriff's pal replied.

A siren pierced the air. Now Ben was convinced a rescue party was in the area. He quietly climbed halfway up the stairs. He was desperate to get out so they wouldn't pass him by, but what if some of those things were still in the house? Did they sleep? He held his breath and listened for any sign the house might still be infested.

As McClellan and his group neared the farmhouse, Lydia Griffin (a meter reader on vacation from Boston) and Sam Miller (a Double-A baseball player from the Pittsburgh area) wandered into their path. One of McClellan's men shot Miller in the back of the skull, while McClellan took care of Lydia personally.

Near the barn, the posse came upon Tim Davidson (a long-haul truck driver on his way to Florida from Michigan). The men in this group were less skilled with their weapons, so more than a dozen shots were fired before a bullet found its way into Davidson's brain.

Closer to the house, Seamus Lynch (on the run for robbery and murder) became tangled in the thick brush. One of the uniformed police officers dispatched Lynch with one well-placed shot, not knowing he'd put down the most wanted man in the area.

At the top of the stairs, Ben felt confident the danger of the flesheaters had passed. But without being able to actually see what was on the other side of the door, caution was still called for. He carefully pulled the two-by-fours out of their cradles and set them aside.

Just as Michael Crane (the *maitre d'* at the one good steakhouse in Evans, who'd stepped outside the back door for a quick smoke) rounded the corner of the farmhouse, a shot rang out. The bullet from McClellan's high-powered rifle entered the back of Crane's head and exited through his right cheekbone. Crane's hands reflexively flew up to his face before his body collapsed on the ground.

"He's a dead one," declared a satisfied McClellan. He shouted to the posse. "Get up here! Nick, Tony, Steve, you wanna get out in that field and build me a bonfire?"

Ben opened the door and cautiously exited the cellar. The dining room was a disaster. Smashed furniture and barricade boards were strewn everywhere in the aftermath of the previous evening's attack. He carefully navigated his way into the room, slowly picking his way around the debris as he made his way to the window…

McClellan called out to one of his men, who obviously needed to be assigned a task. "You," he said, pointing at a downed ghoul. "Drag that out of here and throw it on the fire."

A posse member trotted up to the sheriff from his patrol. "Nothing down here," he said, pointing to a remote area surrounded by trees.

"All right. Go ahead down and give 'em a hand." McClellan turned to Vince. "Let's go check out the house."

Vince already had his eye on the dining-room window. "There's something there." He nodded toward the house. "I heard a noise."

And indeed, a creature was clearly visible through the window, and like all of the ghouls it was staggering back and forth...

Inside the dining room, Ben edged cautiously closer to the window. He could see the search party lined up outside. *Thank God...*

"All right, Vince." McClellan pointed toward the window. "Hit him in the head. Right between the eyes."

Vince aimed at the ghoul and pulled the trigger.

Ben flew backwards, landing on his back with a *thump*. Vince's bullet was buried deep in his brain.

"Good shot." McClellan turned to the posse. "Okay, he's dead. Let's go get him. That's another one for the fire."

EPILOGUE

McClellan and his men entered the farmhouse. The sheriff directed the posse to spread out while he took stock of the dining room. On the floor was one dispatched ghoul. Didn't seem to be in too bad shape, which probably meant he'd died recently. Must be the one Vince shot through the window. *Tough break, buddy...* There weren't any others he could see, but McClellan knew this particular monster wouldn't be the last one they'd take out today.

The four men tasked with retrieval and disposal moved in. They brandished meathooks, which they unceremoniously jammed into the ghoul's torso. McClellan impatiently gestured for the other men to clear the path. The men stepped aside, and the ghoul was dragged from the farmhouse.

Outside, the men pulled the corpse down the porch steps and started the trek across the yard to the pile of ghouls and firewood stacked in the field near the burnt truck. The body jostled and bounced, its arms and legs moving independently of each other as if the men were dragging a marionette instead of a body across the uneven terrain.

"All right, send a wagon through," McClellan directed traffic around the action as ghouls from all across the property were dragged toward the pile. The K-9 unit had just returned from canvassing the field, and the smell of the ghoul from the farmhouse drove the dogs crazy.

"Keep those dogs back off of those things!" shouted the sheriff. *Jesus H. Christ...* He gestured toward a Highway Patrolman who was trying to make his way up to the house. "Come ahead with the motorcycle, please. Let's go!"

The ghoul from the house was hefted up onto the pile of corpses and firewood with all the care and precision of garbage being tossed onto a truck.

McClellan signaled to a posse member who was carrying a can of gasoline. "Hey Randy!" He waved the man toward the bonfire pile. "Light these torches over here."

Randy poured gasoline onto the two torches in the hands of the disposal crew. A lighter was touched to one torch, which burst into flames and in turn was used to light the second torch.

The men touched the flames to the pile of ghouls and broken furniture.

The pile caught fire. The flames spread quickly.

The thing that had been Ben awoke to a state that approached consciousness. Something that might have passed for a thought began to form in its brain: *So hungry... Must feed...* But even that primitive thought was obliterated as the intense heat turned Ben's brain into a syrupy liquid that quickly began to boil away.

The posse went about its business. Soot and smoke spiraled into the air. The creatures and the kindling all burned to interchangeable cinders.

Thirty minutes later, the wind scattered the ashes for miles.

Photo credit: Chad Runyon

ABOUT THE AUTHOR

Sean Abley is an award-winning playwright, screenwriter, journalist, and novelist. He has over thirty plays published by Playscripts, Brooklyn Publishers, Heuer Publishing, Next Stage Press, and Eldridge Plays and Musicals, with titles like *End of the World (With Prom to Follow), The Adventures of Rose Red (Snow White's Less-Famous Sister), Horror High: The Musical* and *Attack of the Killer B's*. His television writing includes multiple episodes of *So Weird* (Disney Channel), *Sabrina, the Animated Series* (Disney/UPN), *Digimon* (Fox Family), as well as several pilots including *Bench Pressly, The World's Strongest Private Dick* with Ahmet Zappa, starring Bruce Campbell. His produced screenplays include the B-movies *Socket, Witchcraft 15: Blood Rose* and *Witchcraft 16: Hollywood Coven*. He was the creator of the "Gay of the Dead" blog on Fangoria.com, and the editor of *Out in the Dark: Interviews with Gay Horror Filmmakers, Actors and Authors*, soon to be reissued by Dark Blue Things Publishing.